Other series by P

LUTHER

This dangerously handsome, effortlessly stylish half-demon is Chicago's foremost paranormal investigator. With magical aptitude and specialized weapons, Luther Cross will handle your supernatural problems... for the right price.

THE MYTH HUNTER

All the legends of the world have some element of truth to them. And to track down those legends, there are the myth hunters. Some, like Elisa Hill, are explorers, trying to learn more about the world. And some are soldiers of fortune, whose only goal is profit and exploitation, no matter the risk.

INFERNUM

A shadowy, globe-spanning network of operatives run by the mysterious power broker known as Dante. They hold allegiance to no one, existing as rogues on the fringes of society. No matter the job, Infernum has an operative to execute it—provided you have the means to pay for it!

VANGUARD

The world has changed. A mysterious event altered the genetic structure of humanity, granting a small percentage of the population superhuman powers. A small team of these specials has been formed to deal with potential threats. Paragon—telekinetic powerhouse; Zenith—hyper-intelligent automaton; Shift—shape-changing teenager; Wraith—teleporting shadow warrior; Sharkskin—human/shark hybrid. Led by the armored Gunsmith, they are Vanguard!

Visit PercivalConstantine.com for an up-to-date list of titles!

This book is a work of fiction. Names, characters, places, and incidents either are products of the author's imagination or are used fictitiously. Any resemblance to actual events or locales or persons, living or dead, is entirely coincidental.

Published by Pulp Corner Press

http://www.percivalconstantine.com

A MORNINGSTAR NOVEL

LUCIFER RISING

BY PERCIVAL CONSTANTINE

FOREWORD

Welcome to *Lucifer Rising*, the first book in the *Morningstar* series. I won't take up a lot of your time at the moment, particularly as you might be sampling this book and want to get to the first chapter. There are generally two types of people who will be reading this book. The first group are people who have read some of my existing books. If you're in that group, then thank you so much for your support, and I hope you enjoy this new book just as much as you've enjoyed the ones in the past.

If you're in the second group, then you have no idea who I am and aren't familiar with any of my other books. So I should let you know right from the start that this book is a spin-off from the six-book *Luther Cross* series which began with *Devil's Due*. If you've never read any of those books, that's okay. I've largely tried to keep this book as accessible as possible for new readers. However, there are some ideas and characters from that series that are referenced in this book. So while you can read and enjoy this book without having ever read any part of the *Luther Cross* series, I think you'll gain a new appreciation for this book if you also get around to reading those titles.

Thanks so much for choosing *Lucifer Rising*. I hope you enjoy it!

CHAPTER 1

In the beginning, God created Heaven and the angels. The angels were beautiful, powerful creatures, holding no free will of their own, existing only to serve their father. But one angel, considered the most beautiful and beloved of all, was so struck by the sin of pride that he sought to elevate his station above that of even the Almighty. He led a rebellion against God, but he and his followers were defeated and cast down into the pits of Hell. His name was Lucifer.

Or at least, that's how the story went. But reality was often quite different from what people had been led to believe. And in truth, the angel known throughout the halls of Heaven as the Morningstar was not so struck with pride that he wanted to be a god himself. The truth of the matter is Lucifer had learned a forbidden secret, known to no other angel save the Seraphim who serve as the priests of Heaven.

There was no Almighty, no Presence, no God. Or if there was, no angel in Heaven had ever spoken to him. Lucifer, honoring his title of Lightbringer, sought to free his brothers and sisters from the bondage of servitude. And so he led a rebellion, but was defeated by his own brother and cast into Hell.

That was where Lucifer had remained, presiding over the Infernal Court and generally keeping to himself for thousands of years. But that all changed when he met a man named Luther Cross. The son of one of Lucifer's lieutenants from the revolt and a human woman. A cambion who saved the world from a rogue angel driven mad by the same knowledge Lucifer had discovered. Lucifer had agreed to help Cross in his campaign in exchange for one thing.

When it was over, Lucifer would walk the Earth and Cross would become the Shaitan, the supreme ruler of Hell.

That was how the Devil found himself in a club located on Chicago's Rush Street, dressed in a white suit and a black silk shirt with an open collar. His dark hair was neatly combed back and his eyes had a haunting yellow glow to them. While the other angels who had fallen with him ended up corrupted by Hell and transformed into demons over time, there was something different about Lucifer. He still maintained his angelic beauty and his feathered wings. The only mark Hell had left upon him was his sulfur-colored eyes.

He moved on the dance floor, gyrating with two women at once. Their hands moved up and down his torso and he felt sensations he hadn't experienced since before The Fall. During his time in Hell, he'd mostly stayed isolated from the others, never indulging his urges. It was a form of penance for him after he failed in his stated mission. As the Lightbringer, he saw himself as a disseminator of truth, but the greatest lie of all was still believed by angels and many humans as well. And after Pyriel's madness, Lucifer realized the other angels would have shared the same fate.

So he declared his penance over and rose to walk the Earth. To experience everything he'd missed out on for centuries. He could feel the perspiration dampen his clothes in a feeble attempt to cool his body. His heart thumped against his chest in excitement as he savored the women's fingertips moving across his arms and chest, their lips softly pressing against his neck.

The song ended, but the women seemed content to continue even without music. Lucifer was tempted himself and was already whispering into their ears, offering the suggestion they find somewhere a bit more private. They both seemed enthused by that idea and Lucifer wrapped his arms around their waists, leading them from the dance floor and towards the exit.

But before they reached the door, a hand fell on Lucifer's shoulder. He turned and saw a large man dressed all in black standing behind him. "If you'll excuse my interruption, sir, but the owner would like to have a word with you.

"Luc, you know the club owner?" asked one of the women.

"How come you didn't tell us?" asked the other.

Lucifer smiled at the two of them, then turned back to the bouncer, his smile vanishing. "I think you've made a mistake, friend."

The bouncer shook his head. "No mistake whatsoever. She was quite insistent you meet with her immediately. *Sire.*" The bouncer's eyes changed yellow, revealing who was truly inside that body.

Lucifer sighed and turned to the women. "I'm afraid I'll have to take care of something first, ladies. If you wouldn't mind waiting at the bar, I promise I won't be long…" he produced a platinum credit card with a wave of his hand and offered it to them, "…and drinks are on me, of course."

They smiled and took the card. Both simultaneously planted a kiss on each cheek before they went to the bar to make use of the credit card. Lucifer smiled with satisfaction as he watched them go, but when he turned back to the bouncer, once more the smile vanished.

"Very well, let's go."

Lucifer was led through the club and up the stairs to the sixth floor. The first floor of Lust was where the main dance floor was. Each subsequent floor up from there was more like an extended balcony wrapped around, with full-service bars, tables, and a view of the dance floor. The sixth floor had one extra feature that set it apart from the rest. And that was a large office with floor-to-ceiling windows looking down at the club. The door was guarded at all times by two men—also demons.

This was where Lucifer left his escort. The two demons bowed their heads as he approached the door and entered. The office was large and spacious. It was colored red and there were burgundy couches and chairs arranged in front of the window with a bar manned by an employee in the far left-hand corner of the room.

Lucifer walked towards the couch and saw a figure sitting there. Long, dark hair spilled over her shoulders and she was dressed in a black suit. She raised a hand without looking at Lucifer and beckoned for him to come. He straightened his jacket and circled around, facing her.

She was a demon as well, named Mara. A loyal servant of Lilith, the first human corrupted by Hell. And now, Mara was Lilith's representative on Earth, ruling over Lust and keeping the demons who managed to make Chicago their home in check. She stared at Lucifer for a few moments, her jaw slackening.

"I...I wasn't sure it was true..." she stuttered, her wide eyes fixed on him. "I mean, I knew. Of course I knew. But to see you here...in the flesh..."

Lucifer chuckled. "It's quite all right. Seems I tend to have that effect on people."

Mara stood slowly, her eyes never wavering. She took a step closer to Lucifer and then bowed down on one knee. Lucifer rolled his eyes and pulled her up to her feet.

"No, don't do that," he said.

"But you're him...the Morningstar..."

"Yes, I know. But one of the reasons I rebelled was because I hated the idea of bondage. Well...*that* form of bondage, at least."

"Right, right...umm..." Mara giggled and played with her hair. She glanced back at the bartender. "You want a...a drink or something?"

"A martini would be lovely. Gin, not vodka."

"Sure, of course."

She signaled the bartender and he went to work making the drink. When it was ready, he brought it over and Lucifer happily accepted the drink. He glanced at the chair nearby.

"May I sit?"

"Oh! Yes, absolutely. Please."

Lucifer settled into the leather chair as he sipped his drink. Mara was still standing and staring at him. She had a reputation in Hell as a fearsome warrior. But now she was acting like a schoolgirl talking to her crush. The whole thing made Lucifer a bit uncomfortable. One of the reasons why he'd isolated himself from the rest of Hell in the first place was because he abhorred being worshipped. He might have been arrogant and prideful, but he certainly was no hypocrite.

"Mara, dear, sit."

"Okay…" she sat back down on the couch.

"Your man said you wanted to speak to me, so I was hoping we could speed things along," said Lucifer. "You see, I have two very beautiful and very aroused women waiting for me at the bar."

"Right, I'm sorry to keep you, but it's just…" She still stammered. "Look, you're…here. On Earth, I mean. And some people—not me, of course—but some people may think that's…bad."

"And what sort of people are we talking about?"

"Well, there's…" She glanced up and pointed towards the ceiling. "I'm guessing they don't like you walking around."

"No, I'd imagine they don't. But they also won't move against me unless I give them reason to," said Lucifer. "Besides, most of their forces are presently focused on monitoring Hell or trying to find that nephilim boy. They won't be an issue."

"And what about others? Like the Sons of Solomon? The Opus Dei?"

Lucifer dismissively waved his hand and took another drink. "I don't concern myself with a bunch of uptight assholes dressing up in robes and jewelry."

"Okay, but what are your plans?"

Lucifer finished his drink and set the glass down on the table. He set his elbows on the armrests and steepled his fingers. "Ever since The Fall, I've been living in seclusion, simply watching from a distance."

"Watching?"

"Hell. Earth. Just watching from my tower. Never interacting, never participating, never experiencing," said Lucifer. "It was because I failed that I felt it was necessary to punish myself with seclusion. But now, I feel like my sentence has been lifted and I want to experience things."

"That's it?"

He nodded. "That's it."

"So you're just here to get drunk and screw anything that moves?"

"I also enjoy sitting on the beach with an interesting book and dinner at a good restaurant. But in so many words, yes." His face softened and he smiled at Mara. "Listen, I'm not interested in making trouble for you or the angels or anyone else in this city. I'm just trying to enjoy my retirement. You can appreciate that, can't you?"

She gave a nod. "I understand. And of course I can. But other people may not feel the same."

"If they cross my path, they'll quickly learn just why I was so feared in Heaven," said Lucifer. "But until then, I do have something to take care of. I trust we won't be speaking of this matter again?"

"If that's what you wish. I apologize if I came off as... over-enthusiastic. I just wanted to be certain all your needs were being met."

Lucifer stood and buttoned his jacket. "Well, not everything. But I'm off to change that. Have a lovely evening, Mara. And thanks for the drink."

He left the office and bid farewell to the demons standing guard. Lucifer quickly went down the six flights of stairs. As he did, someone bumped into him and Lucifer stopped in his tracks. Flashes appeared in his mind's eye, clear as if it were his own memory.

He was looking through someone else's eyes, seeing someone else's memory. Seated at a bar, there was a glass of wine nearby in front of an empty seat. The man whose memory Lucifer was seeing took out a small bottle and unscrewed the cap. He poured some of the liquid into the wine. A few moments later, a woman with brown hair and in a red dress came to the seat and started talking with the man. She picked up the glass and took a drink.

There was another flash. Lucifer saw the woman look drowsy and start to stumble. The man helped her stay on her feet. He suggested they should get some air. She nodded and he started to lead her from the bar, down the stairs.

And that was where the vision stopped.

CHAPTER 2

Contrary to popular belief, the Morningstar was not evil incarnate. Most of what people know about the Devil was just as erroneous as what they knew of the Bible in general. There was no such thing as an ultimate good and an ultimate evil, just varying degrees of each. And though most demons—or even angels, for that matter—would ignore the vision, Lucifer felt compelled to act.

He continued down to the first floor of Lust, but he couldn't see the woman from the vision. As the vision had been from the man's perspective, he had no idea what the would-be perpetrator looked like.

Blindly searching wouldn't work. He needed more leads and he needed them fast. He took a breath and closed his eyes, focusing on the woman's image, committing it to his memory. Then, with his fingers outstretched, he moved through the crowd, brushing his hands against every person as he walked by.

Lucifer wasn't a mind reader, but instead he had a psychometric ability. He was able to see visions through physical contact. His hope was that by focusing on that woman, he would also be able to narrow the scope of his psychometry and find others who had seen where they'd gone.

"Luc! Luc, over here! *Luc!*"

Someone grabbed his shoulder and Lucifer was pulled out of the vision. He spun around, his eyes burning bright yellow and his face contorted in annoyance. But when he turned, he saw the two women who were all over him before, looking at him with horror. Lucifer relaxed and the glow of his eyes diminished.

"Jesus…" said one of the two.

"Not exactly," he replied. "I apologize, but I have something to attend to."

"What?" asked the other. "You're just gonna leave? Thought we were going to party."

"Rain check, I'm afraid. Now if you'll excuse me, I have work to do."

Lucifer turned his back on the women and focused again. Once more, he focused on her image and started moving through the crowd, brushing his fingertips against everyone he walked past. There was nothing at first, no visions. He started to think this was a waste of time.

But then a flash. He saw that same woman with the brown hair and the red dress. She was leaning against someone, a guy in a button-down shirt open down to his chest and his hair loaded up with so much product, it had practically become a helmet. In the vision, Lucifer saw them walk out the front exit.

He stepped outside and saw the man helping the woman into his car. He tipped the valet and got behind the wheel and then took off before Lucifer could get close. Lucifer grunted in frustration and watched as the car drove off, quickly turning on the next street.

"Everything okay, sire?" asked the doorman.

"It will be," said Lucifer, his eyes beginning to smolder.

It worked! That was the thought that kept running through Jeremy's mind as he drove away from Lust. He'd been going to that club for months now, trying to get laid, but always striking out. But that was all about to change. A guy on the message boards he frequented had told him where he could score some roofies. At first, he wasn't going to use them, but then he thought, *why not?*

After all, he was a nice guy. Girls in high school and college would always cry on his shoulder whenever some asshole dumped them. But they would refuse his own advances. So it was really all their fault he was doing this. If they weren't such teases, he wouldn't have to go to such lengths.

So he bought the drug and poured some into the girl's drink. He couldn't even really remember her name. Carrie? Kelly? Cassie? It didn't matter anyway. After tonight, she'd only be remembered by him as that bitch in the red dress he fucked in his car.

But first, he had to find a secluded place. He was nervous about stopping just anywhere. What if some nosy cop was driving down the street? That and finding a place to pull over was pretty hard to begin with. Street parking was lined with cars and he kept turning down side-street after side-street trying to find just one spot. If he was double-parked, that might draw unwanted attention before he could finish.

He turned down another street and his headlights fell

upon someone in the middle of the road. It was a man in a white suit and he had large, feathered wings extending from his back. His eyes burned bright yellow. Jeremy cried out in shock and instinctively pulled the wheel to the side.

The hood of the car slammed into one of the vehicles parked by the side of the road. A car alarm was triggered, which in turn triggered more alarms on the block. Jeremy had hit his head on the steering wheel and when he opened his eyes, his vision was fuzzy. The girl mumbled something from the passenger seat, but still remained unconscious.

Jeremy didn't know what it was he saw, but it had to have been a hallucination or something. Or his eyes playing tricks on him. He didn't remember drinking that much at the bar, but maybe he lost count. Or maybe someone slipped him something, too.

He heard a sound and looked outside his side window. He jumped when he saw the same winged man standing right next to his door. The man bent over and gently knocked on the window.

"Get out of here, you freak!" Jeremy screamed.

The stranger didn't seem to take the hint and just kept knocking. Jeremy shifted the car into reverse and stepped on the gas, slamming his back bumper into a car parked on the other side of the street. When he looked again, the man was gone.

"Fucker," said Jeremy and he shifted into drive, trying to ignore the cacophony of car alarms that echoed up and down the street. He had to get out of here before people on the street woke up and came outside to see what the commotion was all about.

But just as he was about to start moving down the street again, his car was stopped. He stepped on the gas, but the wheels did nothing. It was like he was stuck in the mud. When Jeremy looked in his rear-view mirror, he saw that same freak again, holding onto the back of his car.

"What the hell...?" he muttered. Then, while holding up his phone he screamed, "Get lost before I call the cops!"

Of course he wasn't going to do that. But hopefully it would scare this nutjob off. It seemed like he just vanished. Jeremy turned to drive off, but then he heard a new sound. The sound of metal tearing.

Something ripped his door right off his car. Jeremy looked with horror as that same man stood there, holding the door in his hands as if it were nothing. He bent it in half and then tossed it over his shoulder. He grabbed Jeremy and pulled him from the seat, slamming him against one of the parked cars. As Jeremy looked at him, he saw those yellow eyes burning ever brighter, and the man wore a sadistic grin to match.

"Wh-what the fuck are you?"

"I've had many names over the centuries, Jeremy Raines. But tonight, I'm your punishment."

"P-punishment? But I didn't do anything!"

"I can tell when someone's lying to me, Jeremy. It's one of my many talents. Tell me, have you ever heard of Lucifer?"

"Th-the Devil...?"

"Precisely. And do you know what that name means?"

Jeremy shook his head. This guy was some kind of religious nut. Seemed to be a Satanist. Though he tried to stop it, Jeremy couldn't help himself. He was too scared and he started blubbering, tears welling up in his eyes and his nose quickly filling with snot.

"Please, man...I don't wanna die! I just...I thought..."

"You thought you deserved it. Yes, I know," he said, nearly hissing the words. "I know *exactly* what was running through your twisted little mind, Jeremy. Now answer the question: do you know what Lucifer means?"

Jeremy shook his head, still crying. The stranger just smiled even broader.

"It means 'Lightbringer.' Now this can be interpreted as one who delivers knowledge, but there's also another meaning."

He placed his hand on Jeremy's head and Jeremy could feel heat radiating out from it. At first it was just warm, but the temperature kept rising. Soon, it was as if someone had held a hot frying pan to his face, and his nerves screamed in pain.

"Stop! Please, stop!"

He just kept smiling, his eyes glowing ever brighter. "I think you understand the other interpretation."

He took his hand off and just as Jeremy started to breathe in relief, he was tossed away. Jeremy's back hit the pavement. He didn't even know how far he'd been thrown. But then he opened his eyes and saw the man descend upon him from the sky. He put his foot on Jeremy's chest and kept him pinned down. Even though the guy looked to be slender, it felt like Jeremy was pinned under a car.

"You wear my mark upon your face now, Jeremy Raines," he said. "Every time you look into the mirror, I want you to see my eyes and remember what happened here this night. And if you ever attempt to let your lust override your judgment, rest assured that I *will* return. And next time, I won't be so merciful."

He knelt over again and all Jeremy could see was his

eyes. Jeremy screamed and screamed, retreating into himself.

After he'd finished dealing with Jeremy Raines, Lucifer left the man in the middle of the street, screaming. He stood upright and began walking back to the car. At this point, people had started to come out from their homes, just watching in stunned silence and trying to figure out what was happening.

"It's quite all right, bystanders. Just performing a public service," he said, waving to the stunned onlookers. "I'll be out of your hair in just a moment and then you can return to your evenings already in progress."

Lucifer reached the car and opened the passenger door. He gently took the unconscious woman from the car and held her in his arms. Lucifer lightly placed his hand on her head, concentrating and determining just who she was and where she lived.

"It's going to be okay, Kelly Wright," he whispered. His wings stretched out and wrapped around the two of them. Then, in a flash of yellow light, they vanished.

When they rematerialized, it was in the girl's bedroom. Lucifer very carefully set her down in bed and she squirmed a little, but remained sleeping. She would be fine in the morning, and she'd never know just how bad this evening almost went.

Lucifer stood upright and watched her slumber. He felt pride at what he'd done tonight. Helping someone who no one else would have and punishing someone who likely would have gone on to do it again had he gotten away with it.

It wasn't quite the wild night Lucifer had envisioned for himself, but it brought with it another kind of satisfaction. Lucifer wrapped his wings around himself and disappeared from Kelly's bedroom, as if he'd never been there in the first place.

Tomorrow, there would be tabloid headlines talking of the angel who left a man screaming insanity and took a woman off to Heaven. They wouldn't really know the truth of what happened, but that wasn't important to the Morningstar.

CHAPTER 3

Eden was a real place, but it wasn't a garden as in the Bible. Instead, Eden was a pocket dimension between worlds, separating Heaven and Earth. It was an outpost, from which the angels of Heaven could monitor what humanity was up to on Earth. From there, they could guide the fate of humanity under the watchful eye of an appointed guardian. There were many such outposts, but this was one of the most important.

Anael had never left the safety and security of Heaven. So when she was summoned to Eden, she was more than a little surprised and also fairly curious. She flew from the celestial skies overhead and gently touched down on the veranda just outside the entrance. Her bright, blue eyes peered inside, observing everything. It was in the form of a high-class night club, with shining, white marble everywhere. Her long, dark hair framed the sharp angles of her face and fell lightly on her bare shoulders, ending just before the top of her white dress.

She made no effort to retract her wings, and so when she stepped through the doors, Anael immediately felt all the eyes in the place fall upon her. She looked at them with unease and slowly approached the circular bar in the center of the club. Anael tapped her manicured nails on the marble surface, waiting for one of the servants to come over.

Finally, one of the bartenders approached. He was also staring at her wings and he pointed to them. "Miss, if you don't mind? There's…something of a policy here regarding wings…"

Anael glanced over both her shoulders and then looked at the bartender while sharply cocking her head. "Why? This is an embassy of Heaven, isn't it?"

"Yes, but…" The bartender looked nervous and leaned in closer, lowering his voice. "After recent events, open displays are making people a little…nervous."

"That's not my problem," said Anael. "I'm not here by choice, I was summoned. So I'd rather keep my wings where they are. And if he has a problem with that, then he shouldn't keep me waiting so long."

"I'll just…I'll go tell him you're here. Would you like something to drink while you wait?"

She looked away in something of a dismissive fashion and said, "Surprise me."

"Right…surprise…" He took a stemmed glass and set it on the counter, then filled it with white wine and slid it over to Anael. "I'll go tell him you've arrived."

"You know who I am?" she asked as she picked up the glass.

"I don't believe he's expecting anyone other than you."

The bartender left and started moving through the crowd. Anael picked up the glass and held it up to the light, examining the wine inside. She brought it close to her face and gave a gentle sip. Then, she stuck her tongue into the glass, just barely touching the surface of the liquid. She tried again, testing how the flavor tasted on her tongue.

Satisfied, she took a sip and found she was pleased with the drink.

She went back onto the balcony and looked over the edge, staring into nothingness. It was like this structure floated in a void of endless night. She wondered how any angel could actually be satisfied here, so far from the beauty and wonder of Elysium, the Celestial City.

"Anael."

She turned at the sound of her name and saw a man in a black tuxedo approach. He had short, silver hair and a matching beard. His wings were concealed, but the unearthly blue eyes were a clear indication of his race. He smiled as he approached her and the two briefly embraced.

"It's been a long time, Uriel," she said. "Though I was a bit surprised to learn you were watching over Eden."

"Pyriel made a complete and utter mess of things. Though naturally we've kept things pretty quiet around here, there *have* been rumors circulating," said Uriel.

"Is that the reason you're hiding your wings?"

Uriel gave a sigh and a nod. "Yes. It might seem ridiculous, but Raziel often kept his wings concealed when he was the ambassador here, and many people found it made him more approachable. Pyriel was the opposite, never once hiding them. And his arrogance made things worse. So with all the rumors swirling around after his and Zadkiel's...disappearance and the strange events that occurred last year, I thought it best to lean more into Raziel's example."

"I can appreciate that," said Anael. "Doesn't mean I necessarily approve, but it's understandable."

"That being the case, would you mind...? Just so long as you're in my territory."

Anael rolled her eyes. Her wings started to glow, transforming into pure light and retreating into her back. "There, happy?" She looked away and sipped her drink.

"Thank you," said Uriel.

"Why are you here, anyway?" asked Anael. "I thought Raziel was found again?"

"He and Michael came to an agreement, allowing him to locate the nephilim child without any oversight from Heaven. So he's off with the mother and some others trying to find the boy," said Uriel. "Gabriel would have been the logical choice given his affinity for the mortals, but his role in the Pyriel affair caused some in Heaven to doubt his fealty. So he's been ordered to remain in Elysium for the time being. Michael felt I was a reliable choice to keep watch for now. Though I pray to the Presence they won't keep me here for long."

"So why am here?" asked Anael. "I've never been asked to go beyond the gates of Heaven in all my existence."

Uriel approached the railing and placed his hands on it, leaning over and peering down into the abyss. "There's been another development in the wake of Pyriel's death. One that the Divine Choir wants kept absolutely confidential. Though I'm not sure how well they can do that as many demons are aware of what's happened already."

"What are you talking about?" asked Anael. "What do demons have to do with anything?"

Uriel took a breath and then gave Anael a look of such intensity that she almost flinched. "The son of Abraxas is the new Shaitan."

"What? How did a cambion come to sit on Hell's throne? What about—?" She stopped herself, afraid to utter the name she hadn't spoken in eons. "Was *he* deposed?"

Uriel shook his head. "Honestly? I have no clue. All we know is that Luther Cross now rules Hell. And as for the Morningstar...well..."

Anael's entire body stiffened in anticipation. She moved closer to Uriel, staring into his face, her eyes demanding a clear answer.

"*Tell* me."

Uriel closed his eyes and tilted his head back. "The Morningstar walks the Earth."

Anael felt her legs go weak. She felt like she'd just had all the air knocked out of her body. With her mouth agape, she stared in disbelief at Uriel.

"That's insanity," she said. "It's not possible."

"Unfortunately our sources tell us otherwise," said Uriel. "There was an incident in the mortal city called Chicago. Several witnesses saw a man with wings not far from a den of flesh called Lust."

"Lust?"

"It's run by a demon named Mara," Uriel continued. "The witnesses saw this winged man burn the face of a mortal and left him screaming in the middle of the street."

"That's not proof," said Anael. "That could have been a demon."

"A demon with *feathered* wings?" asked Uriel. "Furthermore, we've been sending mortal spies into Lust to gather information and keep an eye on things. And a few reported seeing a man with the same description as the one with wings. The demons in Mara's employ treated him reverentially, even referring to him as 'sire.' We also know for a fact that Cross is now sitting on Hell's throne while Lucifer is unaccounted for."

"I appreciate the update, but this doesn't concern me."

"The Divine Choir begs to differ," said Uriel. "Of all the Heavenly Host, none knew Lucifer better than you. Before The Fall, the two of you were actually quite close, if I recall correctly. Of course, that was until—"

"I *know* what happened, Uriel, I *don't* need a history lesson!" Anael snapped.

Uriel held up his hands in a defensive posture. "Didn't mean any offense. But the fact of the matter is aside from The Fallen, you understand him best. Maybe even better than they do."

"I *used* to understand him," said Anael.

"Perhaps you should try again. Because you've been selected for this mission and—"

"No," she said.

Uriel's eyes widened in shock. His voice became a harsh whisper. "Have you taken leave of your senses? Do you know what will happen to you if you refuse a mission directly from the Divine Choir?"

"If the Choir wants Lucifer dead, they should summon Azrael out from his cave," said Anael. "But I'm not going to exploit whatever connection may still exist between us just so I can get close enough to knife him in the back."

"So you admit there's still a connection."

She shook her head. "No, I don't. I'm just saying that's what your plan is."

"Well, it's actually not what I had in mind," said Uriel. "I never said I want you to kill the Morningstar. Whether he sits on the throne or not, that would be seen as a violation of the armistice. And after Pyriel nearly brought on Armageddon, we don't want to give the Infernal Court the idea that we're going to break the treaty and start a war."

"Then what *do* you want?" asked Anael.

"Lucifer's arrogance won't let him see the danger in what he's doing," said Uriel. "The demons seem to know, but what happens as more people find out? There's more than just angels and demons to consider, as you well know. What if someone like Thanatos saw Hell as now ripe for the picking?"

"I don't know what you expect me to do."

"Talk to him, try to make him see reason," said Uriel. "If anyone can do it, it's you."

"I tried that once before. And as you'll remember, it didn't work out so well," said Anael. "And when it didn't, you know what I had to do. So if we're going to go down that same path again, then they can just cut to the chase and smite me already."

"That's not it at all, Anael."

Uriel placed a gentle hand on her shoulder to reassure her. It wasn't doing much to help. She still didn't fully trust him or the Divine Choir to keep their word in this instance.

"I understand your trepidation. If it were Michael giving this order, I'm sure he'd want nothing more than for you to deliver Lucifer's head on a stick," said Uriel. "But I'm *not* Michael."

"Don't try to pretend you still harbor some affection for the Adversary."

"You're right, I can't make that claim," said Uriel. "Regardless, I can't just look the other way while he puts a very delicate balance at risk. If there's one thing we've learned from the Pyriel situation, it's that the Host *must* do a better job of policing our own. And like it or not, that also includes Lucifer."

Anael folded her arms and looked down at her bare feet. She was concerned whether or not this was the right move. The way her and Lucifer left things didn't give a whole lot of room for a joyful reunion. In fact, she might be lucky if he didn't kill her on sight.

But if she didn't try, then maybe the Divine Choir would choose someone worse to handle this. And she didn't want to see Lucifer fall a second time, not if there was a chance he could be redeemed.

"I want to be clear on this," she said. "I'm not going to kill him or anyone else, okay?"

"I understand completely, and we're not asking you to do anything of the sort."

"I'll talk to him. I'll try to reason with him. But if I can't reach him, then I just want to go back to Elysium without any trouble," said Anael. "Do we have a deal?"

"I believe we do. Welcome to Earth."

CHAPTER 4

A file was dropped on the desk belonging to Wayne Cooper. The veteran police detective looked up from his cup of coffee at the brown-haired detective who left it for him. She stood there and waited, staring down at the folder. Wayne set the mug back down and turned his attention back to his existing paperwork.

"If you're waiting for a tip, you're gonna be waiting a long time."

"It's one of those weird cases," she replied. "Like that airport thing from when we first met."

"I remember," he said. Janice Wagner used to work out of O'Hare but was recently transferred to the 25th District. The 'airport thing' had involved an immortal opening fire on Luther Cross in the terminal. Janice had been investigating that, until Wayne stepped in.

"Reason I put in for this transfer is because I wanted to work with you, Cooper," said Janice. "So why don't you help me out here?"

Wayne sighed and picked up the file. He looked at the police report. Victim's name was Jeremy Raines. He was attacked in a residential area not far from Rush Street at two in the morning. Witness statements were almost all uniform—woken by car alarms or a crash, and outside right in the middle of the street was a man dressed in white with—

He stopped and closed the folder, then handed it back to Janice. She looked confused and just stared at the file, then back at Wayne.

"What are you doing?"

"You wanted a weird one, that's got weird written all over it," said Wayne. "Take it with my blessings."

"But this is your kind of thing, isn't it?" she asked. "Everyone says to pass these cases onto you."

"Yeah, well maybe I'm looking into changing my reputation around here," said Wayne. "Those weird cases can really bite you in the ass. Believe me, I know."

Janice took the file, but she didn't leave. "Okay, fine. I'll take it. But I still could use some help here."

Wayne sighed and rolled his eyes. "What do you want from me, Wagner? I'm just trying to do my job and keep my head above water."

"The witnesses and the victim all say the same thing—they saw a man in white with giant wings. And they say he burned the victim's face. Then he went to the car where apparently a girl was unconscious and just…poof."

"Yeah, I agree, it sounds fucked up," said Wayne. "But I don't see how I can help you with any of this."

"Humor me, okay? Just one interview," said Janice. "Come with me when I question the victim. You give me your professional opinion and then that's it, you're done."

Wayne looked down at his watch. It was just after eleven in the morning. He finished off what was left of the coffee in the mug, then stood from his chair and grabbed his leather jacket from the back and pulled it on.

"Fine," he said. "But only because it's almost lunchtime and you're buying. You good with that?"

"In exchange for some insight on this, I'll buy you lunch for the rest of the month."

"Just be careful what you wish for, Wagner. After we're finished with this, you may want to turn back the clock. This kind of shit can get pretty damn crazy and not everyone is equipped to handle it."

"Trust me, I'm not everyone," said Wagner. "I'll drive."

"Damn straight you will, I'm not about to waste my gas on some wild goose chase," muttered Wayne.

At Northwestern Memorial Hospital, Wayne watched Jeremy Raines through the vertical blinds on the room's window. His face was bandaged and he stared off into space. His lips were constantly moving, but Wayne couldn't hear what was being said.

"Coop?"

Wayne turned around when Janice called his name. A woman in a white coat stood beside her with a badge clipped to her breast pocket. She was in her mid-forties and wore wire-framed glasses.

"This is Dr. Sandra Martinez," said Janice, motioning to the woman. She then introduced Wayne. "Doctor, Detective Cooper here is consulting with me on Mr. Raines' case."

"Anything I can do to help," said Martinez.

"How bad are the burns?" asked Wayne.

"Just surface, really. But Mr. Raines isn't still here because of the burns."

"What do you mean?"

"Mr. Raines has suffered a severe psychotic break, I'm afraid," said Martinez.

Wayne took another look at the doctor's badge. "You're a psychiatrist?"

Martinez nodded. "The burns weren't the problem and most of the injuries he suffered were minor at best. Under normal circumstances, he would have been released already."

"But this isn't normal," said Wayne. "Has he said anything?"

"He hasn't *stopped* talking," said Martinez. "But it's hard to make sense of what he's saying."

"What *has* he been saying?" asked Janice.

"He goes through moments of lucidity. But one thing he talks about are his assailant's eyes."

Wayne perked up at that. "What about the eyes?"

"He said the eyes weren't human. You'd think the wings he mentioned would be what frightened him the most, but no—it was the eyes."

"What color were they?"

Martinez furrowed her brow. "I'm sorry?"

"He said the eyes were inhuman. What color did he say they were?" asked Wayne. "Red?"

Martinez was staring at Wayne as if he were the one who needed a psychiatrist. And then after a beat, she shook her head. "No, actually. He said they were yellow."

"Yellow..." Wayne sighed. He knew that meant a demon. But why would a demon do something like this? "What about the woman? Did he say anything about her?"

"As a matter of fact, yes." Martinez sighed. "The EMTs found a small, empty bottle among the possessions he had on him at the time. There were traces of Flunitrazepam inside."

"What's that?" asked Wayne.

"Rohypnol," said Janice with a disgusted look on her face. "He drugged her."

"That's even stranger…" muttered Wayne, turning back to look at Raines through the window.

"Unfortunately not that strange," said Martinez. "In some of his more lucid moments, Mr. Raines admitted he picked up the woman at a night club nearby."

"I don't suppose you remember the name of it?" asked Janice.

"I can't recall off the top of my head, but I'm sure I have it written down in my notes—"

"Lust," said Wayne without turning from the window.

"You know…I think he's right," said Martinez. "I'm fairly certain that was the name."

"Did he say anything else about the attacker?" asked Wayne.

"One other thing," said Martinez. "He said it was the Devil."

"Would you mind if we spoke with him?" asked Wayne.

Martinez checked her watch. "Just briefly, okay? He needs to rest."

Wayne went to the door and entered the room. Janice followed behind him and they both approached Jeremy's bed. He was still staring off into space, his lips never once ceasing their movement. But they couldn't hear anything coming from his mouth.

"Mr. Raines?" asked Wayne. "My name's Detective Cooper, this is Detective Wagner. We're investing the man who attacked you."

Jeremy's mouth stopped moving. But he wouldn't look at them. Wouldn't say anything, either.

"I just want you to explain to me in your own words exactly what you remember about this man," said Wayne.

Jeremy didn't respond. Wayne moved closer so he was now in Jeremy's line of sight. And even though the young man was looking right at Wayne, the detective felt as if Jeremy still wasn't really looking at anything at all. Wayne moved his hand in front of Jeremy's face and there was no real response. As if he was living in his own world.

"Mr. Raines—Jeremy—I know you may think you can't explain what you saw. That you think no one will believe you," said Wayne. "But I want you to know that I've also seen some pretty unbelievable things."

"Have you?" asked Jeremy, now finally speaking.

But he still seemed lost in his mind. Jeremy reached out and took hold of Wayne's wrist. Janice moved to react, but Wayne gave her a look that told her it was okay. Wayne focused on Jeremy once more. Jeremy lifted Wayne's hand and brought it to the bandage, laying it gently on top.

"I felt his touch…" said Jeremy, tears beginning to well up in his uncovered eye. "The Devil branded me."

Wayne pulled his hand away and cleared his throat. "Did he say anything?"

"He called himself the Lightbringer," said Jeremy. "He warned me—if I ever tried again, he would be back. He marked me, so I would always remember."

Jeremy reached for the bandage and pulled it off. Wayne and Janice were both stunned to see the burns on his face in the shape of a hand.

"Do you see, Detectives?" asked Jeremy. "The Devil is here. And he's vengeful."

After leaving the hospital, the two detectives went to M Burger, which was just down the street, for the lunch Janice promised to buy. They sat at one of the outdoor tables. Janice bit into her Chicago Double and stared at the Impossible Burger sitting in front of Wayne as he sipped his drink.

"Surprised a guy like you would order a burger that's not made of meat," she said.

"Why's that?"

Janice shrugged. "You strike me as one of those old-fashioned cops."

"You know what they say about assumptions," said Wayne. "Truth is, I haven't touched meat in about ten years."

"You watch one of those documentaries about the food industry or something?"

"No, nothing like that." Wayne shook his head. "My father died of a massive coronary when he was my age. And he was definitely an old-school meat-and-potatoes guy. So I decided it was time for a change."

"What do you make of Raines?" she asked.

"He saw something. But the Devil…?"

"You think he really *did* see something supernatural?"

Wayne did. But despite Janice's enthusiasm to learn more about this world, he wasn't entirely convinced she was ready to know everything. About angels and demons, Heaven and Hell, and all the other crazy shit that went down in this city once the sun went down.

"Well, one thing's for certain—Raines got off light," said Janice. "Roofies a girl and then takes her into his car.

Pretty clear what he was planning to do. Maybe this guy was actually an angel instead of a demon."

"That's a good point..." muttered Wayne.

Why *would* a demon care about a soon-to-be rapist? Luther once told him demons fed off negative energy and enjoyed corrupting souls, so wouldn't it be better for one to let Raines go through with what he had planned? There was also the matter of the wings, which sounded very strange, too. Luther had told Wayne of demons with wings, but they usually kept them concealed. And this one had feathered wings, but Luther said demonic wings were more like a bat's.

"I'll be right back, I have to make a call." Wayne stood from the table and went around the corner so Janice was out of earshot. He took out his phone and called Luther's number. It had been months since they last saw each other, and Wayne had been chilly towards him. Not without reason, but Wayne still felt a pang of guilt over the situation. This would at least give him a chance to bury the hatchet.

"The number you have dialed is no longer in service."

Wayne furrowed his brow when he heard that message. He tried Luther's number again and got the same result. Why would Luther change his number suddenly? Wayne searched through his contact list and found the number for one of their mutual acquaintances. He called it and waited until he heard a feminine voice answer.

"Tess, it's Coop," said Wayne. "I was trying to get in touch with Cross but had no luck."

"Coop? You mean you didn't hear?" asked Tessa. She was a witch based in Chicago and the two of them worked together a few times.

"Hear what?" asked Wayne.

CHAPTER 5

Father Alan Gibson entered the nave of the Shrine of Our Lady of Pompeii and saw there was one man sitting in the pews. Gibson walked down the aisle between the pews and approached the front one, where the man just sat. He didn't seem to be in prayer, he was just sitting there and staring. He was dressed in a sweatshirt with the hood pulled up over his head, which also sported a baseball cap.

"Can I help you, son?" asked Gibson.

The man didn't answer. The combination of visor and hood kept his face in shadow, so for all Gibson knew, the stranger may have been sleeping. His clothes didn't look dirty, so Gibson assumed it wasn't a homeless man trying to find a place to sleep.

"Excuse me..." Gibson reached a hand to gently shake the man's shoulder. But before he could make contact, the man suddenly looked at him. Gibson jumped at the action. He sighed and relaxed.

"I'm sorry. Did I startle you, Father?"

"Just a bit, but that's all right," said Gibson. "Is there something I can help you with?"

"Oh, I don't think you want to help me." He returned

his attention to the altar and just stared at it.

"I would be happy to help you." Gibson pulled his sleeve up to show his watch. "But it's after 6:30 and that's when we close. However, if you're free tomorrow morning—"

"You'll help me tomorrow?"

"Yes, of course. We open our doors at—"

"But I thought the church was supposed to welcome God's children at any time."

"Yes, well unfortunately, some of us still need sleep."

"But Father..." The man stood from the pew and faced Gibson. Once again, the priest was startled and nearly jumped back. The man took a few steps closer. His face was still a mass of shadows. "I would very much like to confess my sins."

"Then you could come back tomorrow."

"Are you sure you can't accept my confession now? I'm worried what will happen to my soul if it has to carry this burden for one more day."

"That's not really how it works. So long as you accept responsibility for your actions, you'll know forgiveness. How long it takes you to confess isn't as important as how sincere your confession is."

"But please, Father. I'm having trouble sleeping."

Gibson sighed and checked his watch again. He didn't like driving home too late at night, but this probably wouldn't take too much time. One confession wouldn't keep him here that long, after all. He nodded.

"Okay, I'll hear your confession."

"Oh, good. Thank you, Father."

The man started walking to the confessional and Gibson followed. They both entered their respective booths and Gibson waited for the man to begin.

"Forgive me, Father, for I have sinned."

"Tell me of your sins, child," said Gibson.

"I think God has cursed me, Father."

Gibson furrowed his brow. "And why do you think that?"

"Because I've been having these urges lately. Urges that I know are bad. Evil, even."

"What sort of urges?"

"Well, just this morning I was on the train. And I saw a woman displaying far too much flesh."

"And this brought up lustful thoughts?"

There was a pause, followed by a low chuckle. The laugher was like the babbling of a creek and it caused the hairs on Gibson's neck to stand on end.

"I'm sorry, is something funny?" asked the priest.

"Oh yes, quite funny, as a matter of fact," said the man. "You would like that, wouldn't you, Father? To hear my lustful thoughts? To hear about how I wanted to bend that harlot over and have my way with her? Right there with the rest of the Blue Line passengers for an audience? I'm sure you'd enjoy hearing all about how I fantasized of making her scream as I raped her."

"I beg your pardon?"

"How does it usually work, Father? You go into the confessional and you hear all the sick, twisted fantasies of your precious flock. Do you beat the bishop under your robe while you're listening, or do you just store those naughty little tales up in your spank bank for later?"

"I think I've had about all I can stand of this!" said Gibson as he rose to leave the booth. "Now you can get out of my church right now or I'll call the police!"

"No, wait! Please, Father..."

Gibson paused and just listened. It started soft at first. And then it grew louder. The man was openly weeping in the booth. What was the proper reaction here? The priest wasn't sure, but he chose to sit back down and give the man at least a few more minutes.

"I'm sorry, Father. But it's like I told you, the Lord has cursed me."

"How do you think he cursed you? These impure thoughts?"

"No, you just heard it. That wasn't me speaking to you," he said. "That was the demon he put inside me."

Gibson had listened to as much as he could tolerate. Now he knew this was probably just some prankster. More proof of how this world was being dragged down to Hell itself. No one had any respect anymore. Not for institutions, not for God, not even for themselves.

"I think we're done here."

"But Father, the demon says if you don't stop me, then it will happen again."

Again, Gibson found himself pausing. "What? What exactly did the demon say would happen again?"

"He'll make me do it..." said the man and then began sobbing once more. "He'll kill again."

"You've...*killed* someone?"

"No!" the man protested. "It's not me, I swear! It's the demon! That woman I told you about, he made me get off the train and follow her. We followed her all the way to her apartment. And then...we forced our way inside."

Gibson reached into his jacket pocket to find his cell phone. He still wasn't sure if this guy was telling the truth or if this was all some sort of revolting prank. But he also knew he couldn't take the risk. If it turned out this man *was* a killer, then Gibson had to inform the authorities. He activated his phone's voice memo app and started recording.

"What happened then?" asked Gibson. "What did the demon make you do?"

The man broke into sobs again. He was blubbering so loud that Gibson couldn't make out anything he said. It was all just gibberish. He'd have to call the police, let them know that this was one sick individual. Maybe he wasn't a killer, but he clearly needed help.

"Oh, Father."

The man's tone changed. It grew darker. More confident. And it had an edge to it. Just like the laughter from earlier, it completely unnerved Gibson. Just what exactly was he supposed to say to this guy?

"There you go again, you naughty boy," said the man. "Trying to learn all my deepest, darkest secrets for your own perverted pleasure. But I'm afraid you won't get any of that from me. You see, I never had relations with the woman, forced or otherwise. But I *did* cut her open from stem to sternum."

"My God..."

"I rubbed her organs and her bodily fluids all over my naked body and pleasured myself right there in her living room as her lifeless eyes watched."

Gibson went to the phone app and started to dial. He had hit the first two numbers, but before he could hit the third, the man spoke again. And this time, what he said chilled Gibson far more.

"Father, are you trying to call the police on me?"

"N-no, of course not..."

"I know when you're lying, Father. I can sense it. Just

as surely as I can smell the fear exuding from every pore of your meat."

Just as he was about to make the call, a hand burst through the door of the booth. The man's strength was unreal and Gibson's ability to speak was frozen by the terror he felt. With the door ripped off, the man now stepped into the booth.

And now, Gibson could see into the darkness that once kept the man's face completely shrouded. Those his features were still a mystery, one thing that was clear as day were the bright, glowing eyes within the heart of that darkness. They burned bright yellow, just as Gibson imagined the fires of Hell must be.

"You know, Father. Confessions are supposed to be private," said the demon. But now, you've gone and betrayed your most sacred vows. I'm afraid that will require a punishment all its own."

The screams of Father Alan Gibson echoed throughout the church, and possibly even filtered out to the surrounding streets. Yet if anyone did hear them, no one gave any indication of it. Gibson screamed for as long as he was able.

But eventually, everyone stops screaming.

CHAPTER 6

For his home on Earth, Lucifer had selected a large estate in Evanston's Lakeshore Historic District. It was a revitalized Tudor-style mansion, right across from the lake. Despite the easy access to a beach, it had a pool of its own, which was what the former King of Hell was currently enjoying.

He'd done a few dozen laps already across the length of the fifty-foot pool and hadn't even begun to feel any sort of fatigue. In fact, it was likely he could continue doing laps all day without a moment's rest needed. But not only would that have bored him eventually, it also would prove rude towards the guest who just arrived and cast a shadow across the sunlit pool.

Lucifer stopped at the pool's edge right beneath the shadow. He dunked his head beneath the water and re-emerged, wiping the water from his face and sliding a hand back through his dark hair. He looked up with yellow eyes. The sun was obscured by the woman who stood before him, its light highlighting the edges of the large, feathered wings. Blue eyes were fixated on him, twinkling like stars.

He expected the them to send an errand boy at some point. He just never expected it would be *her*.

Lucifer climbed out of the pool and she averted her eyes when she saw he wore no swimming trunks. He showed no sign of shame or embarrassment as he strolled over to a small patio table. Standing under the shade of the umbrella, Lucifer began to dry himself off with a towel that had been on the table.

"Ana, it's been a long time," he said.

"My *name* is Anael," she said. "*Nobody* calls me Ana."

"Not anymore, at least…" he muttered in a hushed tone. "I thought you didn't care much for Earth. Or me. So to what do I owe this pleasure?"

She still refused to look at him, turning around completely and resting her hands on her hips. "Could you put on some pants first?"

"I don't remember you being so shy in the old days," he said with a slight grin.

"A lot's changed since then," she said, and then added, "Adversary."

"Still picking at old wounds," said Lucifer. "Very well." He snapped his fingers and there was a flash of light. It faded almost as fast as it formed and he was now fully clothed in black slacks and a burgundy button-down shirt. "Is that better?"

Anael was almost afraid to turn around, half-convinced he'd still try to mock her. But she did and felt a bit of relief when she saw he was indeed fully clothed. "Much better, thank you."

"Those wings make you a bit conspicuous you know," he said. "Why don't you fold them? I *do* have neighbors."

"Unlike you, I'm not ashamed of my true nature," said Anael. "And your yard is surrounded by walls. No one can see us."

"As you wish." Lucifer pulled the patio chair out from under the table and rested in it. He motioned to the other chair. "Why don't you sit then and we can reminisce?'

Anael approached the table, but she didn't sit on the chair properly. Instead, she perched on its back. Her long, white dress draped over her knees, its hem casting a shadow over her bare feet.

"Do you really think I'd come all this way just for a social visit? Especially given what you did?" she asked.

He sighed. "I suppose that was too much to hope for, wasn't it?" Lucifer looked down at his hand, the fingers gently tapping on the armrest. "The Choir sent you. Didn't they?"

"Not directly. I was summoned by Uriel. He's now overlooking Eden."

"Is that so?" asked Lucifer. "I would have thought Gabriel would accept that post."

"Apparently, the Choir felt he'd grown too…attached to humanity. And it was determined he should spend some more time within Elysium."

"Ahh yes, mustn't allow too much independent thought to develop," said Lucifer. "Might turn into another me."

"You started a civil war that caused the deaths of an untold number of angels. Pyriel tried to start a second war here on Earth," said Anael. "I'd say a little less freedom is a good thing."

"If only you knew how ridiculous you sounded…" muttered Lucifer, following it up with a chuckle.

"So now I'm ridiculous?" asked Anael. "Wanting to preserve peace is ridiculous? Wanting to maintain balance in the universe is ridiculous? We are *angels*."

"No, *you* are an angel. I stopped being that when I fell."

"Then why do you still have wings, Adversary?"

"A cruel joke. Taunting me for what I used to be, for how I bought into the propaganda," he said. "And I have a name as well."

"Yes, you do. One which I vowed to never speak again," said Anael. "Your betrayal stung some harder than others. You talk of old wounds, but just hearing your name opens them up for me."

"That was never my intention," said Lucifer. "I asked you to come with me. To join me."

"And I told you I wouldn't believe your lies."

"I never lie."

She scoffed. "*Everything* you say is a lie."

"I've only ever told you the truth. You've just never been able to accept it."

"We're not going down that road again," said Anael. "The Choir has a message for you—return to Hell."

Lucifer sat in silence for a few moments. Anael wasn't sure if he was actually contemplating what she said or just refusing to answer the question. Then he stood from the chair and walked up the marble steps to the veranda. Anael flew after him, landing and following him through the back door of his mansion.

"Where are you going?"

"Normally I don't drink before noon, but you seem intent on spoiling my mood."

He strolled through the house and came to a library. There was a large fireplace between the book cases, all of which had their shelves filled to capacity. Anael couldn't help but marvel at the collection. Not only that, but the furniture as well. She wondered how he could have managed to furnish this entire home and curate a library of his own in so short a period.

Lucifer went over to a liquor cabinet and fixed himself a martini. "I'd offer you one as well, but you won't be staying very long."

"Is that your way of saying you plan to kick me out of your house?" she asked. "How *did* you manage to get all this so quickly?"

"Online shopping is a wonderful thing," said Lucifer. "Amazing what you can do on this planet when money is no object."

"Just how many of the deadly sins have you broken since you rose?"

"That's actually a good question." Lucifer settled into a large, leather chair near the fireplace. He set the martini glass on a small table by the side and then started counting on his fingers. "Let's see now... Lust, definitely guilty of that... Greed, I think a case could be made for it... Gluttony to an extent, if you count imbibing copious amounts of alcohol... Envy of mortals is what led me to resign my post in the first place, as did sloth..."

"Wrath," said Anael. "I heard about the man you attacked."

"Ahh yes, the would-be rapist."

"That's the sort of problem the Choir has," said Anael. "The armistice between Heaven and Hell was quite clear on interfering in Earthly affairs."

"Indeed it was clear," said Lucifer. "It was between the Divine Choir and the Infernal Court. I'm not a part of either. I'm simply another fallen angel."

She folded her arms and glared at him, her blue eyes darkening. "Others won't see it that way. You're the father of demons. You're their leader. More than that, you're their deity."

Lucifer wagged a finger as he sipped his martini. "No. I *never* asked for that. I didn't want to be the ruler of Hell nor anywhere else for that matter. Not once have I ever considered myself a deity of any kind."

"Then what was the purpose of your betrayal?"

"*We* were the ones betrayed, Ana."

The use of that nickname again spurred something within Anael. Her blood ran hot. Her arms dropped to her sides and her fingers unconsciously curled into fists. She looked away from him, her jaw tightening.

"I *told* you not to call me that."

"I only did what I've always done. The very thing I was *made* to do—disseminate knowledge."

She had trouble restraining her anger. "You were made to spread the word of the Presence and the glory of the Host, not to foment treason."

"I tried to expose the *lie* that we were only meant for servitude." Lucifer set the drink down and rose, moving closer to Anael. "We are so much more than the Seraphim ever gave us credit. Just like mortals, we're capable of emotion, of independent thought."

Anael pulled away from him and held up her hand, pointing a finger at the Morningstar. "Not another word! I'm done with this blasphemy!"

"You know I'm right."

"Stop!"

The azure color of soulfire sparked around Anael's hand. And then in an instant, flared out, forging into a sword that was held right at Lucifer's neck. He raised his hands up in a gesture of peace and took a step back. But

Anael's heart was racing. She was dizzy, her head swirling.

"You see?" asked Lucifer. "Emotion."

Anael retracted the soulfire blade back into her form and turned her back on Lucifer. She breathed deep, trying to regain her composure. Something about him always had that effect on her. She hated the way he made her feel. But at the same time, this brief exchange was more exhilaration than she'd experienced in over a millennia.

"Of the two of us, you were always the most passionate," said Lucifer. "It was from you that I learned how to experience emotions."

"There's one sin you forgot to mention." She looked at him again. "Pride. Uriel was right about you, your pride has completely overtaken whatever remained of logic in that twisted consciousness of yours."

"There's nothing twisted about me, An—" He stopped himself. "Anael."

He had no reason to enrage her once again. His point had already been proven, and he was in her head now. She knew it, too. Now he would play the diplomat. Try and appeal to her in another way. Before The Fall, it was always said that no angel in Heaven had a sweeter tongue than the Morningstar.

"Amazing you can say that and believe it," she said. "Your grace is well and truly depleted. Possibly in the negatives."

"Some simply choose to follow their own path. That alone doesn't make them twisted."

"That's your pride talking again. You've always been incapable of accepting responsibility. It's why you isolated yourself in Hell. And it's why you ran away to Earth."

"Hell is in good hands. Cross can keep an eye on things

down there very effectively," said Lucifer. "Perhaps even better than I ever could."

"He's *not* the Adversary." Anael pointed once again. "*You* are."

"Only because I was forced into that position." He then scoffed. "For all I know, perhaps the Choir wanted it that way. Having a villain to point to sure makes it a lot easier to rally the masses to your cause. And it avoids embarrassing questions the Seraphim don't want to answer."

"More blasphemy. I shouldn't be surprised," said Anael. "Your presence here is going to cause problems, Lucifer. More problems than you can begin to imagine."

"You have no idea what you're talking about."

"Time will tell," she said. "Time will certainly tell. Until then, you can rest assured that I'll be keeping a watchful eye on you."

"Just do me the courtesy of teleporting as opposed to flying off my front lawn," said Lucifer. "Mrs. Gordon next door is a fairly annoying neighbor as it is. I'd rather not have to explain winged women taking off in front of my house."

Anael wrapped herself in her wings and began to glow with a blue light. In a flash, she was gone. Lucifer returned to the table and retrieved his drink, taking another sip of it. Now that she was in the mix, things suddenly became a lot more complicated.

Which seemed exactly what the Choir wanted.

CHAPTER 7

Wayne ducked under the crime scene tape and walked up the steps to the church entrance. A uniformed officer opened the door and allowed him in. A chain around his neck suspended his badge right above the navy button-down he wore under his leather jacket. He took a pair of latex gloves from one of the CSI and entered the church's nave. Most of the attention was around the confessional.

He walked through the nave and approached his colleagues. A crime scene photographer was shooting images of the body and one of the uniformed officers rushed past Wayne, covering his mouth and obviously trying to hold in his lunch.

"I'd say 'good morning,' but that doesn't seem appropriate right now," said Wayne.

Janice was kneeling over the body and she stood once she heard Wayne's voice. He rolled his eyes when he saw her standing there and she just scoffed in response.

"Don't give me that look. You knew I was going to be here."

"Here I was hoping you would have come to your senses," he said. "What's the story?"

She glanced back at the body. "Alan Gibson, he was a priest here. His eyes were gouged out and the killer left coins over the sockets."

"That's not all," said the CSI tech, rising from the body. He came over to them looking clearly disturbed. "There were holes in his hands and feet, a gaping wound in his side, and what look to be claw marks around the cranium. I think he may have been alive when the wounds were inflicted and then left to bleed out."

"Also found his phone in the confessional," said Janice. "There's a recording on it, but we haven't listened to it, yet."

"Was he tied up?" asked Wayne.

The CSI shook his head.

"Then why not call for help? Why just sit there until you died?"

A shrug was the CSI's response. "Maybe he passed out from the shock?"'

"Or maybe the killer waited until he died," said Janice. "But that'd be crazy, right? It's not like this is a secluded place. Even if the church was closed, it's too big a risk of exposure."

"Unless he has nothing to fear," said Wayne.

"*Or* she."

"Statistically, most serial killers are men," said Wayne.

"We don't know if this is a serial yet," said Janice. "A serial killer can only be identified if there are at least three victims—"

"I know the technicalities, Wagner," he said. "But look at all this. Do you know what those wounds represent?"

She shook her head.

"Stigmata," said Wayne. "It's when a person experiences the same wounds that Jesus experienced during the Crucifixion. Holes in the hands and feet, scratches around the head, and a side wound where he was stabbed by a spear. There are stories throughout the centuries of extremely devout Christians suddenly experiencing some or all of these wounds. Consider that, plus we're in a church and the victim's a priest. This has all the markings of a ritual killing. And whoever did this probably isn't going to stop with just one."

"What about the eyes? And the coins?" she asked.

"Bible talks about an eye for an eye. And placing coins over the eyes was done so the deceased could pay the ferryman of the River Styx," said Wayne. "Was there anything unusual about the coins?"

"Just regular old quarters," said Janice. "No significance there, I assume?"

"Not that I know of."

"There's something else you both should see," said the CSI. He walked over to the confessional and opened the door. Scrawled in blood on the back wall were four numbers with a period separating them.

"1.263," said Janice, reading the numbers. She glanced at Wayne, who was staring at them. "You have any clue what that means?"

Wayne stepped closer to the confessional, trying to piece the numbers together in his head. He couldn't think of anything and finally could do nothing other than shake his head.

"Assuming your ritual theory is true and this is a religiously motivated killing, then maybe the numbers refer to a Bible verse."

"Possible, but no book is referenced. And Biblical

citations tend to use a colon to separate chapter and verse, not a period," he said.

"Maybe he was absent the day they taught that in English class."

"I think it's something else, but what, I don't know," said Wayne. "No witnesses?"

"None. This probably happened after the church closed. He was found by one of the staff this morning. We tried to question her, but she's still in a state of shock."

"And you said something about a recording?"

"Yeah. His phone was left unlocked," said Janice. "Also strange. Who doesn't have their phone set to auto-lock?"

"Someone who wanted us to listen to that recording," said Wayne. "Let's play it, there might be something we can use."

The CSI passed the phone to Janice. She produced a stylus from her jacket pocket and used it to operate the phone with her gloves on. Janice hit play on the voice memo and they all listened to Gibson's confession. Both voices were men and Wayne almost wanted to rub it in that he was right, but chose to remain silent.

The recording began with Gibson asking what the demon made him do. The man taunted Gibson and described killing someone else—a woman. Then, the man accused Gibson of trying to call the police. The recording ended with Gibson's screams.

The entire thing was gruesome, and clearly the killer wanted them to hear that. Both Janice and the CSI looked unnerved by the recording. Wayne was, too, but not for the same reason. Yes, it was objectively horrible to listen to. But even worse than that was what Gibson said at the beginning.

"What did the demon make you do?"

Was the killer actually possessed by a demon? Wayne had assisted Luther with cases like this in the past, but when he called Tessa, she informed him that Luther was no longer available. And she had also said she was out of state on another job. He didn't know how to contact Alistair Carraway, plus it seemed unlikely the old exorcist was still in town anyway.

Another thought had occurred to him—Lust. That was the club where Jeremy Raines picked up his intended victim and was scarred by some sort of angel. Now this. The timing of these two different events could have been completely coincidental. But there was also the possibility they were connected.

"What are you thinking?" asked Janice.

"I'm thinking I've got someone I need to talk with," said Wayne.

"You have a lead on this? *Already*?"

"Just a hunch for the moment. Might be nothing, but maybe it could help us." Wayne took off the latex gloves and moved over to the confessional and took a photo of the numbers."

"Well naturally I'm coming with you," she said, handing Gibson's phone back to the CSI.

"No." Wayne stopped and faced her. "Like I said, this might be nothing. And my source isn't really comfortable with cops, so you being there might make them even twitchier than normal. Besides, someone's got to do more legwork on this case. Talk to the woman who found Gibson's body, look into his background and see if he has any enemies. Also look into the woman he mentioned on the recording, see if there are any recent cases that match. We've got very little to go on right now, so let's try to narrow it down a bit."

"I know you're stonewalling me."

"Honestly, I'm not," said Wayne. "Please, just help me out. If this amounts to anything, you'll be the first person I tell."

He left the church and jogged down the street to where he'd parked his car. Lust would be closed now, but Wayne knew there was an apartment above the club. He only hoped whoever Luther left in charge of that place was a friendlier sort of demon.

Though the notion that any sort of demon could be called friendly was something he found difficult to swallow to begin with.

Mara's body fought her attempts to open her eyes as the screeching sound of a ringing bell pierced her sleep. The room was fairly dark, but even the filtering of some sunlight through the heavy curtains was enough to nearly blind her. Her mouth was dry and as consciousness came to her, she felt the pleasant welcome of a massive headache.

She sat up in bed. There was a naked woman next to her and on the floor, a naked man. Both of them still sound asleep. She pulled the silk sheets off her body and went to the closet to retrieve a robe. Mara tied the belt as she groggily moved through the apartment and to the front entrance. It led to a stairwell that was connected to the back of the club, so it wasn't often she got visitors.

"Whoever the fuck this is, you'd better have something worth saying. Otherwise I'm going to peel your skin off and turn you into a leather coat."

She unlocked the door and pulled it open, fully ready to claw out the eyes of the person with the audacity to wake her up. On the other side of the door was Wayne Cooper, one arm braced against the frame, hunched over slightly and looking at her with intense, blue eyes.

Mara yawned and leaned against the door. "What do you want, pig?"

Wayne scoffed. "See you've been catching up on pop culture. You're running Lust now?"

"What's it to you?"

"I've got an interesting case. One that I think might be right up your alley."

Mara chuckled and then became serious. "Do I *look* like a fucking cambion? You see me walking around with ancient daggers or magic pistols? Just because Cross isn't around now doesn't mean you can just ask the closest demon to do your job for you."

She started to close the door, but Wayne stopped it with his foot. Mara groaned and opened it wider. "Move the foot or it becomes my trophy."

"This is serious. I think I might be dealing with a demon going on a killing spree," said Wayne. "I'm not asking you to team up, just to answer a few questions about the case."

"Why should I bother with that shit?" she asked. "I'm nursing a hangover that makes torture in Hell seem like a Sunday afternoon picnic. And I've got a newlywed couple in my bedroom that I plan to defile just a little bit more before lunch."

"Ten minutes, it's all I ask," said Wayne. "Once I've asked my questions, you have my word that I won't bother you again."

She sighed. The thought of answering some mortal's inane questions about demons sounded about as pleasant as a root canal. But on the other hand, she still had a boss to answer to and it was her job to keep the demonic population in check. So she'd humor him for the time being.

"Ten minutes, that's all you get. Then you either leave willingly or I throw you out the window."

Wayne stepped inside the apartment. "Do you have any coffee?"

"Coffee is for guests, not dick cops who interrupt my orgies."

"Fair enough." Wayne stood in the foyer with his hands in his pockets and looked around the apartment. The foyer was connected to a living room, with a couch and a television and not much else. A kitchen was off to the side and straight ahead, he saw the door to the bedroom ajar and a figure moving on the floor. Obviously one half of the couple Mara had mentioned.

"So talk. What's this all about?"

Wayne quickly filled her in on the details of the case. Mara leaned against the wall and listened with her arms folded over her chest. She was struggling to find anything in the detective's description that would even slightly pique her interest, but she came up with nothing.

"So what do you think?" asked Wayne once he finished. "Could it be a demon?"

"Yeah, could be," said Mara. "Could also just be some nutjob in his grandma's underwear. I've only been up here a short time and one thing I've learned so far is that humans are capable of just as much depravity as the most corrupt demon—possibly even more."

"I hope you're right about that," said Wayne.

Mara cocked her brow. "Most people would find that more disturbing."

"I've been a cop for over thirty years, I know what's out there in the dark. And as terrifying as humans can be, at least they can be stopped with a bullet," said Wayne. "Maybe if I still had some supernatural help, I'd feel differently. But I don't."

"No, you don't," said Mara. "Be sure to remember that the next time you need advice. Now if that's all…"

"Actually, one more thing."

Wayne reached into his jacket and took out his cell phone. He brought up a photo of the numbers they found scrawled on the back of the confessional and showed it to Mara. She rolled her eyes as she took the phone from him and looked at the picture.

"Think it's pretty obvious he's religiously motivated. These numbers are the only other lead we've got. The killer wrote them in the priest's blood, so I assume it's a reference to some kind of religious text. I'm sure you're not a big Bible reader, but maybe you know something about them. Because I've never seen a Bible citation like that."

Mara scoffed and tossed his phone back to him. "That's because it's *not* a Bible citation."

"Then what is it?"

"1.263," said Mara. "Book 1, Line 263. It's a poetry citation."

"Oh, great," muttered Wayne. "That sure as shit narrows it down."

"It's *Paradise Lost.*"

"You're sure?"

"That line's a pretty famous one," said Mara. "'Better to reign in Hell then serve in Heav'n.'"

Wayne sighed. "Great, that doesn't ominous at all..." He reached into his jacket and took out a business card. "If you come across anything—"

"I won't."

"*If*, consider giving me a call." Wayne set it down on a small table near the door and then took his leave.

CHAPTER 8

Hell wasn't what mortals thought it was. It wasn't just a giant torture room engulfed in flames. But rather, a metaphysical realm with various territories ruled over by the different Hell Lords. Most of whom were lieutenants in Lucifer's rebellion against Heaven. All Lucifer sought in his rebellion was freedom, and as such he allowed each of his lieutenants to rule over their territories as they saw fit.

As a result, some of the territories were indeed places of torment. But others were places of despair. A few were nothing but chaotic, engulfed in endless war. And some simply existed.

Hell itself was not a prison, and yet even the Morningstar understood the need for such a place. It was the deepest level of the pit, a place of eternal ice. Those who were unfortunate enough to find themselves in that place were kept in a state of suspension—unable to move, unable to interact, and yet fully conscious the whole time. It was where those who threatened the delicate balance achieved through the armistice with Heaven were sent. Its name was Cocytus.

And like all prisons, this one had a warden as well. He

was a demon with an exoskeleton of twisted and pointed bones. His head took on the appearance of a goat's skull, with the horns twisting out from the sides of his head and peeking through the hood of his heavy cloak. Yellow embers burned in the blackness of the eye sockets as he looked out from the banks above the frozen sea, a staff held in one hand.

He sensed a presence and turned. Another demon, albeit much more humanoid in appearance, approached the jailer. His head was smooth and his physique muscular. Batlike wings protruded from his bare back and his ears were pointed, his eyes bright yellow.

"Good day to you, Belial," said the jailer.

"Why did you summon me, Erebus?" asked Belial.

"We have a situation. One which I believe your master would like to be informed of."

"The Morningstar has taken a leave of absence."

Belial's response was almost a growl, and Erebus noticed it. "Something not sitting well with you, my friend?"

"Know your place, jailer," said Belial, eyes flashing with anger.

"I'm sorry if that was out of line," said Erebus. "But regardless of the Morningstar's absence, this is important."

"Take it to the Infernal Court and their new king," said Belial. "Lucifer is gone."

"Lucifer is the one who wanted Cocytus to be created in the first place."

"As a necessary evil, yes. To contain the likes of Lilith and Abraxas. And as such, he needs to know what has happened as I believe his actions have triggered it."

"Just what sort of nonsense are you spouting?" asked Belial.

Erebus moved from the banks and walked over the ice. He extended his arm and with a bony finger, beckoned the demon to follow. Belial didn't trust the ice, so his wings raised him above the ground and he flew closer. He suspended himself in a hover just above the ice. Erebus' finger moved and pointed to the ice below.

"Observe."

The warden struck his staff against the ice. Cracks spidered out from the point of impact, growing in number and intensity. And the ice fell out beneath them. Erebus began to fall and even though he had his wings, Belial found himself being pulled along. Yet they weren't quite falling. It was more of a controlled descent, moving slowly down a path that tunneled right through the frozen sea. In the ice surrounding them, Belial could see the prisoners kept in Cocytus. Their bodies were frozen in time, but their eyes were moving and he could see the despair and hatred in all of them.

"Where are you taking me, Erebus?" asked Belial.

"Here."

They suddenly stopped, suspended in the air. Erebus placed his skeletal hand on the ice and it began to glow, the light spreading out through and illuminating the prisoners within. But then Belial could see what Erebus wanted to show him. There were cracks deep within the ice. Big caverns where once someone had been contained. Chains and shackles that were left broken and mangled.

"Do you see now?" asked Erebus.

"Yes, I believe I do." Belial had never really known fear before. But he couldn't deny the feeling of unease that started to form in the pit of his stomach. "What happened, jailer?"

"If only I knew," said Erebus. "But some of those imprisoned in Cocytus have somehow managed to free themselves."

"And you think that has something to do with Lucifer?" asked Belial. "How is escape even possible?"

"Lucifer created Cocytus, using much of his own magical reserves. That magic is tied to him, his presence. And when he abdicated the throne and left Hell, Cocytus' connection to him weakened," said Erebus. "So yes, I believe this is certainly tied to him. That weakness allowed cracks to form in the prison."

"How many have escaped?"

Erebus shook his head. "It's impossible to say. But some of the most dangerous demons in Hell are now roaming free somewhere in the realm. And if they've managed to escape into Hell's territories…"

"They'd be like any other demon," said Belial. "And they could have the capability to make their way to Earth."

"Now you see why I summoned you," said Erebus. "Lucifer must be warned about this. Not only do we need him and his magicks to strengthen Cocytus and prevent further escapes, but there is another issue. If the Divine Choir learns of these events, then this crisis caused by Lucifer's abdication could indeed constitute a violation of the treaty."

"And thus hold the potential of another war. The very thing Lucifer tried to prevent when he created this place," said Belial. "So what exactly would you have me do?"

Erebus raised his hand and snapped his fingers. Reality warped around them and once more, they stood on the banks of the frozen sea. Belial seemed slightly disoriented at first, but quickly recovered.

"I would have thought your task is plainly obvious," said Erebus. "Go to Earth. Find the Morningstar. Inform him of what's happened and tell him he must take whatever steps necessary to fix this."

Belial groaned. He despised Earth and the talking monkeys that infected it. He even despised other demons, which was why he enjoyed spending his time finding new ways to torture them. But he was loyal to Lucifer and Lucifer alone. He would have to find his master and see to his protection. Right now, the Morningstar was at risk of becoming a target of not only Heaven itself, but whatever demons wished for revenge against the king who imprisoned them.

CHAPTER 9

Willis Tower was the tallest building in Chicago and at one point, the entire world. Reaching it from Evanston would take forty-five minutes to an hour by car or public transportation. On foot, the walk would be over four hours. Lucifer didn't need to waste that kind of time. His wings not only gave him the ability to fly, but to walk between different planes of existence. That allowed him to travel from his mansion to an alley nearby in the blink of an eye.

The wings transformed into energy and receded into his back. He tugged on the cuffs of his black shirt, then straightened his white jacket and circled around from the alley to the front entrance. With his hands in his pockets, Lucifer pushed past the other people in the lobby and got into the elevator before any of them. A snap of his fingers caused the doors to close much faster than they normally would. Standing in a small metal box crammed in with others was not his idea of a good time.

Lucifer examined the buttons for the various floors. He then put his finger in a spot above and began tracing it in a deliberate pattern. His lips began moving, whispering an incantation in a barely audible voice. A white button shimmered into existence and Lucifer pressed that.

The elevator sped rapidly through the shaft, and the display with the floor indicator went out of control, unable to recognize where the elevator was. Bright, white lights started filtering between the doors and the buttons all flashed in a strobe-like effect.

It all came to a sudden stop and the doors opened, revealing the large, white club of Eden. Lucifer calmly stepped from the elevator and as soon as he did, every bit of chatter came to a stop. All eyes fell on him. They all knew who he was and his very presence in this place put every last one of them on edge.

That just made the Morningstar smile.

He wasn't here to make friends. He had another agenda in mind. Lucifer walked through the club with confident, deliberate steps. As he passed the pianist—a beautiful woman in a red dress—he stopped and walked over to her.

"And you are?" he asked.

"S-Scarlett," she said, staring up at him with large, green eyes.

"An appropriate name." He offered his hand. "My name is—"

"Lucifer..."

The way she whispered his name was almost as if it were forbidden. But she couldn't help reaching for the offered hand with her own. And once she did, Lucifer gently tugged on it as he bent over. His lips brushed against the surface of her knuckles. When he looked up at her again, he saw her cheeks had reddened.

"A *very* appropriate name, it would seem," he said. "Perhaps after I've completed my business here, you and I could step outside for some pleasure."

"I—I—"

Scarlett was interrupted by a voice that bellowed throughout the silent hall. It spoke Lucifer's title, but without fear. Instead, there was an obvious hint of anger running through that voice. Lucifer released Scarlett's hand and turned to face his opponent.

Uriel's wings were unfurled, azure fire barely contained within his eyes. His arms were stiffly held at his sides, hands curled into tight fists. Lucifer just smiled at the display of dominance and calmly moved closer. He came right up to the angel and gave him a playful pat on the chest.

"Zip up, Uriel. You're overcompensating," he said. "Besides, I didn't come here for a pissing match."

Uriel's anger seemed to only grow with that comment.

"Easy there, Mr. Servant of Heaven," said Lucifer, clicking his tongue. "Wrath is a particularly nasty sin as I recall."

"You have no permission to enter this place," said Uriel. "You are *not* welcome here."

"Clearly, permission isn't required, otherwise I wouldn't be here," said Lucifer as he sauntered out to the balcony. He hopped on the railing and perched himself there, facing his former brethren with his arms resting on bent legs. "After all, not just anyone can enter one of these embassies."

"What are you doing here, Adversary?"

Uriel moved closer, albeit slowly. If he were a snake, he'd be coiled. He was ready to pounce at the slightest provocation. And Lucifer was sorely tempted to test the angel. Part of him felt it would have been justified if he did. This choir boy was screwing with his life and he wouldn't have any of it.

"I had a visit from an old friend this morning," said

Lucifer. "You sent my Ana after me."

"She's *not* yours, she never was," said Uriel. "And her name is Anael."

Lucifer's grin faded. "It stings, doesn't it? To know what her and I had. Is that what this is all about, Uriel? You're still sore over losing to the better man after all this time?"

Uriel became a blur and crossed the divide between them in an instant. His hand grabbed Lucifer's throat and pushed him off the balcony, holding him over the abyss. Soulfire started to crackle around his fingertips. But as for the Morningstar, the grin returned to his face.

"Touched a nerve, did I?" he asked.

"You chose your path, Morningstar," he said. "It was *your* decision to lead a revolt against the Host. To turn brother against brother. And you got what you wanted—a place where you could rule over as you please."

"Rule was never what I wanted, Uriel. And I'm done sulking about it, isolating myself and watching eternity pass me by."

"You have responsibilities," said Uriel. "Your abdication puts all of existence at risk."

"And who told you that?" asked Lucifer. "The Choir?"

"It doesn't matter who—"

Lucifer's wings unfurled to their full span. He pried Uriel's hand from his throat and hovered under his own power.

"As a matter of fact, it does," he said. "Since the beginning, the Choir has spread lies in order to maintain control. I've decided to stop playing their game and that terrifies them. So they now say that by stepping off the chessboard, I've created a dangerous situation. It's all done in the name of preserving me as the boogeyman for you and the rest of the puppets in Heaven. And do you know why?"

"No, but I'm certain you have your own bullshit theory to share," said Uriel.

"Indeed I do," said Lucifer. "The Choir made an example of me and the rest of The Fallen. They needed an enemy to point to. And there's no greater enemy than the Morningstar, is there? Cross may be ruling Hell, but he's still just a cambion. And the rest of the Court, they may be fallen angels, but they weren't the ones who led the revolt. No, they need *me*. If they allowed you to believe I could just give up and stop playing, what would that do for others who have tired of the games?"

Uriel scoffed. "With all the hot air in that head of yours, you don't even *need* wings. Though I have to admit being impressed that anything could keep the weight of your ego off the ground."

"You wasted your time sending Anael. No one, not even her, could convince me to return to Hell." Lucifer hovered over to the balcony and touched down. His wings retracted and he slid his hands into his pockets. "When I tell you I'm not interested in playing these games anymore, I mean it. Let the Choir have Heaven, let them manipulate humanity. All I ask is to be left out of it."

He moved closer to Uriel and held out one of his hands. Uriel studied Lucifer's face and looked down at the hand. His posture started to relax a bit, the tension leaving his body. The wings seemed to sigh as they slackened, folding gently. The angel began to reach his hand out…but then he slapped Lucifer's away.

"You think I'm gullible enough to fall for one of your tricks?" he asked. "I sent Anael because once upon a time, she could get you to listen to reason."

"You tried to exploit the spark we once shared. But that was extinguished by betrayal."

"You have no one to blame for that but yourself," said Uriel. "I'm commanding you, Lucifer. By decree of the Divine Choir itself, the highest authority in all the universe. Return to your post or suffer the consequences."

Lucifer's face darkened as his eyes smoldered. He moved in closer and his wings flared to life once more, reaching their full span.. When it came to displays of dominance, Uriel had nothing on him. And the Morningstar could sense the angel's dread beginning to grow.

"The last time the Divine Choir tried to force me to do their bidding, they had to send an army after me," said Lucifer. "What can *you* hope to accomplish, Uriel?"

Uriel took a moment to regain his composure before he said, "Last time, you also had an army. And even then, you lost."

"There are no armies in play now. The Choir wouldn't dare. Not without triggering another war."

"Say it came down to that," said Uriel. "The Choir still has the Host of Heaven backing them up. Legions of angels. But you? You gave up your throne and your seat on the Infernal Court. If the Choir were to bring the full force of the Host down upon your head, would any of your former lieutenants even back you up?"

"It's a gamble," said Lucifer. "But I'm not opposed to games of chance. Are you?"

Uriel shook his head. "You're bluffing. You wouldn't put yourself at that kind of risk."

"Try me."

Lucifer's wings retracted as he spun on his heel. He winked at Scarlett while passing her on his stroll to the elevator. All the other eyes in Eden still studied him. The silence had extended throughout his conversation with Uriel. Once he entered the elevator, he locked eyes with the angel, the two of them glaring, waiting for the other to blink first. The doors closed before either did.

One thing was certain—Uriel was nervous about locking horns with him. But the truth of it was that Lucifer himself worried over just how far the Divine Choir would take this. If push came to shove, would they really come after him in full force? And if that happened, what if Uriel was right? What if the Morningstar no longer had any followers in Hell?

He couldn't think about that. All he had to do was keep them at bay. If need be, he'd stay on the move, keep himself cloaked and one step ahead of them. They couldn't destroy what they couldn't find, after all.

CHAPTER 10

Lucifer had scarcely been home for more than twenty minutes when he heard the sound of the doorbell. He sighed and placed the game controller on the coffee table and rose from the couch. Two visitors in one day, both of them uninvited. If this was becoming a pattern, he'd have to end it before it got out of hand.

There were a few possibilities for who might be ringing his doorbell at ten o'clock at night. Anael would have been the obvious one, though she would more than likely just barge in uninvited as she did that morning. Mara was the other likely candidate—she still viewed Lucifer as her lord and savior even though he'd always rejected such worship. Possibly even a friend of Cross. Other possibilities entered his mind. And of all those potentials, the demon he laid eyes on when he opened the door certainly wasn't one of them.

There was a bit of a pause before Lucifer said, "Beli-al…?"

"M'Lord." Belial gave a bow from the front porch. "May I enter?"

"Stop standing on ceremony. Of course." Lucifer opened the door wider for his onetime soldier.

Belial strode inside and scanned the foyer. "So this is what passes for accommodation on Earth?"

Lucifer shut and locked the door. "Am I to take it you don't approve?"

"No, the house is fine." Belial turned and looked at his master. "Other things aren't."

Lucifer's eyes rolled up as he went back into the living room. He jumped over the back of the couch and landed on the cushions. Belial followed him in and stood behind the couch just as Lucifer resumed his game.

"What *is* that?" he heard the demon ask.

"It's called a video game," said Lucifer. "A way to alleviate stress."

"Seems pointless."

"You say that like it's a bad thing," said Lucifer. "I was created to serve the Seraphim, Belial, and then I was forced to rule over Hell. I came to Earth with the express goal of a pointless existence."

"Might want to reconsider that."

Lucifer's character climbed into a sports car and began speeding through the streets of the virtual city. "No, I don't think I will."

"Though I hate to be the one to tell you, things are not well downstairs."

"Cross can handle it. I wouldn't have appointed him if I thought otherwise."

"I'm not so sure he can. And this isn't about Cross, it's about you."

The car weaved in and out of the lanes, with Lucifer's thumbs expertly maneuvering the vehicle. He took a sharp turn, almost narrowly colliding with another car, then kept on going.

"Sit down and pick up a controller," he said.

"I'm not here for meaningless games."

"Then order a pizza. Or we can watch a movie," said Lucifer. "But one thing we're *not* going to do is discuss whatever's happening in Hell. I've had enough celestial talk for one day."

"I wouldn't have come myself if it weren't important. You know how I feel about Earth."

"And I'm sure you believe that. But what you keep failing to grasp is that I couldn't care less."

"I've spoken with Erebus."

For Lucifer, the game seemed to slow to a crawl. His car collided with another and flipped over it, crashing onto the ground and turning a few more times before it exploded into flames. The screen went black and the controller fell onto the ground. A moment passed before Lucifer picked it up again and hit the pause button.

"Erebus." He repeated the name. And his voice even went up a bit at the end, as if confirming what he'd just heard.

"Yes." Belial circled around and stood in front of the TV. "Cocytus has weakened. And some have escaped."

"Who?"

"Erebus isn't sure of who. Or how many," said Belial. "All he knows is that they're free. And it's connected to you."

Lucifer dropped the controller and stood up. He left the living room and went into the kitchen, then opened the refrigerator and took two bottles of Goose Island beer. One he offered to Belial, who had followed him again. He pulled the cap off the other and started to drink it while leaning against the kitchen island.

"Erebus believes that—"

"That because I created Cocytus with my own power, my abdication has now weakened its barriers," said Lucifer. "Yes, I know."

"We need you back, sire," said Belial. "You have to fortify the walls of the prison before more escape."

Lucifer looked down and then took another drink. There was a sudden tightening of his chest. It all seemed crystal clear to him now. But back then it didn't. He was in too much of a rush to leave it all behind and start over. And now he was being faced with the consequences of his rash decision.

"I can't…"

"What?" asked Belial. "What do you mean you can't? You *have* to. I understand you and Cross made a deal, but some things are more important. Creation of Cocytus after all was one of the terms of the armistice."

"And these escapes could be seen as a violation. Yes, I'm well aware," said Lucifer. "But you don't understand, Belial."

"You're right, I don't. I followed you all those eons ago because I believed in what you were trying to do. To give us something other than servitude. And now when we need you possibly more than ever, you refuse. You abandoned us, Lucifer. Abandoned me."

Lucifer's chin fell towards his chest. There was a thickness in his throat. "I can't go back. I *won't*."

Belial's eyes were cold. He picked up the bottle of beer and looked at the label. Then he threw it right past Lucifer's head. It shattered against the hard surface of the refrigerator and the contents splashed everywhere. Lucifer shook off the beer and flecks of glass that had struck him.

"A bit extreme, don't you think?"

"I trusted you. Gave up everything for you. We *all* did. And now another war is on the horizon because of your actions. Except this time, you refuse to lift a finger to stop it."

Lucifer took a deep breath and slowly let it flow past his lips. "You're right. You should know what my reasons are." He took another drink before beginning to tell his story. "When I created Cocytus, I used a considerable amount of my own essence to do so. Power on that scale…it's something no angel had ever done before. Possibly since."

Belial's shoulders sagged. "What are you saying, my Lord?"

"Stop calling me that," said Lucifer. "I'm nobody's lord. I never wanted any title."

"I apologize. I'll try to see it doesn't happen again," he said. "But what do you mean?"

"Say I went back to Hell. Took the throne again. I'd only be half of what I once was," said Lucifer with a dejected breath. "Maybe less."

Belial shook his head. "You mean you can't fortify Cocytus."

"No." Lucifer took another drink and braced himself against the island. He stared down at the marble countertop. "That power I used, it's not something that can be replenished. It's one of many reasons why I kept myself isolated from the rest of Hell's denizens. I didn't want you all to know just how much my power had been depleted by that act."

He wouldn't allow himself to look at Belial's face. This was once a promising young angel, one who had sacrificed everything because he believed in what Lucifer stood for.

And now, he was able to see just what his former general had become.

"Hell is better off without me, Belial," said Lucifer. "I just want to live my life and forget about the past. I've already had far more brushes with it lately than I'd care for."

"Perhaps you've earned a respite from celestial matters. And if it were up to me, I would happily grant that to you," said Belial. "But it's not. I came here because I had no other choice. Even if your power has waned, this is a responsibility. You built Cocytus and the demons that have escaped will not simply move on with their lives. These are creatures considered too extreme for Hell itself. Surely there must be something you can do."

Lucifer finished the beer. His eyebrows rose as his gaze finally found Belial's once more. The Morningstar stood up straight, his posture stiffening. "Maybe there is."

Belial reached and scratched the back of his bald head. "You know something? Remembered something perhaps?"

"Cocytus brands the soul, leaving a permanent mark on it. It means that a part of Cocytus is carried within that brand. It's not something that can be removed."

"You can track it?" asked Belial.

Lucifer sighed and glanced away. "Nothing so specific. But I can get a general sense. Though it will require some extra materials that I don't have access to here."

"You're saying we need assistance," said Belial.

The Morningstar gave a nod. "Cross has allies here, but I'd rather not get them mixed up in this. And also, we'd need magic of a darker sort."

"And who in this place would have access to magic like that?"

"I know someone, but we can't simply walk up to him.

He's become far more cautious these days and we'll need someone to make an introduction."

"Who?"

"Mara," said Lucifer. "Now that she runs Lust, she has her finger on the pulse of the supernatural underworld. And like you, she still has reverence for me. She has the connections I'll need."

"Very well," said Belial. "So when do we start?"

Lucifer's eyes met the demon's. "Belial, you've done enough. You told me what was happening, you forced me to confront my own shame. You can return home content in the knowledge that I'll finish this."

Belial folded his arms over his broad chest and fixed his gaze. "I think you know I'm not about to do that, sire."

"If you truly think of me as your lord, then you'll do as I command."

His head very slowly and deliberately turned from side to side, never breaking eye contact for a second. "With all due respect, sire, shove your commands. You said it yourself—you aren't as strong as you once were. And the demons of Cocytus, they'll be fueled by rage after all that time imprisoned in the worst Hell has to offer. You *will* need my help on this."

Lucifer's shoulders tensed. This was his mess and he had to clean it up. He didn't want anyone else getting mixed up in this more than they already had. Even going to Mara was something he had no desire to do. But when Belial set his mind to something, he hardly ever wavered. There would be no convincing him to stay out of this, that much had quickly become obvious.

There was another matter to consider—Belial was absolutely right. Lucifer's strength was not what it once was.

Enough to teach a would-be rapist the error of his ways, sure. But to take on the demons that Cocytus once held in its icy grip was another story. Whether or not Lucifer's pride would allow him to admit it, he couldn't do this without some kind of backup.

"I know how much you hate it here," said Lucifer.

"That hasn't changed. But I also swore an oath to the Morningstar. And I plan on fulfilling that obligation. If you would have me, I would be honored to serve alongside you once more."

"And if I say I don't want you?"

"Then I'm coming anyway. Free will, right? Isn't that what you taught us?"

Lucifer's lips curled up in a smile of satisfaction. It seemed at least some of The Fallen had embraced what he fought for all that time ago. There was something to be said for that.

"Very well, it's your funeral. Let's get started. We have a club to hit and some demons to locate."

CHAPTER 11

The alleys surrounding Rush Street were more or less quiet and dark. Until, of course, a bright flash of light signaled the arrival of Lucifer and Belial in one of them. There weren't many in the area, so few noticed. The ones who did quickly dismissed it. Lucifer's wings converted to light and receded into his back. Belial went to the mouth of the alley and looked out. His shoulders were tense and he stood just a little hunched. Lucifer moved slowly behind him and tapped his servant on his arm.

"What are you doing?"

"Isn't it obvious?" asked Belial. "I'm scanning the area for any threats to your person."

Lucifer rolled his eyes and pushed past the demon. He could hear Belial's footsteps chasing after him as he crossed the street. Threats to his person—it was such an absurd statement. The only thing that could really harm him was one of the other angels and none would risk coming after him, not without violating the armistice. He had nothing to fear.

There was a crowd gathered outside Lust, just the same as any other night. Lucifer strolled up to the front door, breaking through the line, and the bouncers gave him a bow before opening the door. There were protests coming from those waiting to get in, but Lucifer just ignored the noise they made and entered.

"Sire, this is dangerous," came Belial's voice from beside Lucifer. "It's risky for you to go out into the open without securing the area first."

Lucifer gave a sigh and looked at his companion. "Belial, I'm the Morningstar. I held my own against the greatest warriors Heaven had to offer. I think I can take care of myself."

"That may be so, but remember what you told me at the house?"

"Of course I do, but not being *as* powerful as I once was is *not* the same thing as being powerless," said Lucifer. "And besides, this is a den of sin owned and operated by demons. What should I fear in a place like this?"

Lucifer turned from Belial and slithered through the throng of people to reach the bar. He beckoned the bartender over with a finger. When the bartender looked at Lucifer, his eyes flashed yellow and he bowed.

"Tequila sunrise." Lucifer looked over his shoulder. "Care for a drink, Belial?"

Belial's face had reddened and his eyes bounced from one part of the club to another, seeking out any potential threats. "No."

Lucifer gave a shrug. "Suit yourself, my friend." He looked back at the bartender. "Just the sunrise. And let the master of the house know that I'd like a word with her in private."

"Of course, sire," said the bartender. He quickly prepared the drink and set it on the counter, then excused himself to go make the call to Mara.

Lucifer took the sunrise and turned towards the dance floor, leaning against the bar as he sipped the yellow and red mixture. He twirled the stirrer around, watching as the colors slowly merged together. A memory was triggered. He rapidly fell through a swirl of warm colors, playing across his eyes in a kaleidoscopic fashion. His skin sizzled and popped and the stench of burning features overwhelmed his nostrils. Falling. Faster. But no matter how fast he fell, it wasn't enough to extinguish the flames. And deep below him, he saw the end. Absolute darkness. And when he finally hit the bottom, the flames spread out from his body, igniting everything around him and revealing the barren wasteland in which he'd now found himself.

"—ey! I'm talking to you!"

The pained voice pulled Lucifer from his memory. He looked up from the flame-colored drink and saw a man standing right in front of him. His lips were tight and his nostrils flared as he shouted over the music. But as far as Lucifer could remember, he'd never seen this man before.

"I'm sorry," said Lucifer. "Is there something I can help you with?"

"Is there something *you* can help *me* with?" His voice shook as he repeated Lucifer's question.

"Yes, that's what I said."

It happened so fast that Lucifer didn't even see it coming. A stinging pain through his face accompanying the *smack* of knuckles striking his cheekbone. The glass was knocked over, and the fiery mixture of orange juice, grenadine, and tequila spilled over the counter. Others moved away and Lucifer reached a hand for where he was struck. The punch wasn't that strong, not even enough to draw any blood.

"I'm sorry, I think you may have me confused with someone else, my friend," said Lucifer. "So I suggest you apologize, buy me another drink to replace the one you forced me to knock over, and then go about your business."

The man held up his left hand to draw attention to the gold band around his ring finger. "You *are* my business. You slept with my wife, you sonnuva bitch!"

He came at Lucifer again. This time, the Morningstar saw the punch coming and easily moved out of its path.

"And how do you know I'm your man?" asked Lucifer.

"Last week," he said. "She was here with a bachelorette party. I came to pick her up, but when I got here, I saw her get into a cab with *you*."

"Now, I'll admit, that *does* look bad," said Lucifer. "But I hardly see how *I'm* responsible for the actions of your wife."

"She didn't come home until the next morning! When I confronted her, we got into a fight and she walked out!" His voice grew louder, almost shrill. Shallow breaths with clenched fists and teeth. He was going to strike again.

"I'm sorry, friend," said Lucifer. "But maybe if you'd been a more attentive lover, she wouldn't have found the need to go out and find someone else."

He screamed and charged again. But before he could make contact, he was grabbed from behind. Belial wrapped his arms around the man's torso and kept him restrained. The demon growled as his eyes hummed with power.

"Wh-what the hell *are* you?"

"Precisely," said Belial as he flipped the man over and slammed him onto the ground.

That drew even more attention from the patrons and Lucifer didn't want things to escalate too far. There was something in the man's face. Past the anger, Lucifer could see the watering of his eyes. He was in pain, absolutely heartbroken over what he'd lost. Something stirred deep within the Morningstar, a reminder of a pain he himself had once experienced over betrayal.

"Belial," said Lucifer. "Let him up."

"But sire—!"

"Did you hear what I said? Let. Him. Up."

Lucifer's tone sharpened, but his voice didn't grow a single octave. It was clear Belial understood his master's anger, though, because he pulled the man up to his feet and set him upright. Lucifer moved closer to the man and reached a hand for him, brushing against his cheek.

"It's Doug, isn't it?"

His head cocked to the side and his jaw slackened. It was almost as if he hadn't heard Lucifer at first. "How did you know—"

"That's not important," said Lucifer. "I understand you want someone to blame. But I didn't make Lily do anything. That's not how I operate. She came with me of her own free will."

"Bullshit, she'd never—!"

"I don't lie, Douglas. And if you truly love her, then I think you should have a long talk with her about what happened. Find out why she did what she did. And try to find it in your heart to forgive her."

Doug's mouth opened silently. Part of him looked like he wanted to rip Lucifer's face off. But another part seemed convinced that Lucifer was indeed being honest with him.

"You have a question, I can tell," said Lucifer. "Go on."

"How can I forgive her after this?"

"If you love her, how can you not?"

He stared off into space, then the ground, and finally his eyes found Lucifer once more. "Why are you telling me all this?"

"Because for what it's worth, I'm sorry," said Lucifer. "As hard as it may be for you to accept, I actually understand a little bit of what you must be going through. Now, go on. It seems you have some thinking to do."

Doug's movements were sluggish, as if he was trying to remember how to walk. He staggered away from Lucifer and the crowd of people backed up, clearing a path to the door. When he reached the entrance, he looked at Lucifer one final time. But the gaze was distant, as if he were just waking from a nightmare. He turned and went out the doors.

Lucifer took a breath and went to the bar. "I don't suppose I could trouble you for another sunrise?"

"Y-yes, of course, sir."

Once the drink arrived, Lucifer picked it up and immediately took a sip. Belial sidled beside him.

"Humans and their monogamy." Belial gave a scoff. "Such a strange concept. Why they develop these strong bonds over mashing their genitals together is a mystery to me."

"Doesn't surprise me to hear you say that. You were never one for companionship to begin with, old friend," said Lucifer.

"And you are?" asked Belial. "You who spent most of eternity keeping to yourself in your tower?"

"Yes, I did go through quite the dry spell. Perhaps why I'm now making up for lost time."

Lucifer's eyes took in the sight of the people swaying to the music. Their movements were hypnotic, fueled by lust and alcohol. And perhaps other chemicals as well. Men and women alike, freely indulging themselves in the pleasures of the flesh. He closed his eyes and inhaled deeply, smelling the pheromones that hung in the air like moisture on a humid day.

"And what's so special about these mortals?" asked Belial. "I'm sure someone like Mara would be perfectly happy to engage in carnal relations with the Morningstar."

"I'm not interested in demons, Belial. Their emotions are mostly fueled by Hell's corrupting influence," said Lucifer. "No, I'm after purity."

"I doubt any of the mortals you'll find in here are virgins."

Lucifer gave a chuckle. "That's not what I meant. I'm talking about purity of emotion. It's what drew me to the men and women I've already slept with. And it's what drew our friend Douglas to strike me."

"I still don't understand why you didn't let me kill him for you. In the old days—"

"Yes, in the old days, I would have happily allowed you to butcher him with my blessings," said Lucifer.

"That talking monkey assaulted you. And yet *you* were the one to apologize." Belial shook his head. "It doesn't make any sense why you would do such a thing."

"He had good reason to be angry."

"If his woman were satisfied, she wouldn't have gone looking elsewhere for her sexual gratification," said Belial. "Or maybe he was just jealous that she was able to find someone else to mash her genitals with while he was incapable."

"That could be true. Regardless, he was hurt by my actions. And even if he drove his wife into the arms of another, it's clear he wasn't ready to take responsibility for his role in it."

"He should learn some responsibility. If you allowed me to, I could have taught him some responsibility."

"No, you would have simply broken him in half and he'd hardly learn anything from that."

"Why do you defend him?"

"I suppose I can't say I blame him. In fact, a part of me even relates to him."

"In what way? Since when do you relate so much with human emotions?"

Lucifer stared into the drink, the memories of the fire flashing through his mind's eye once more. And the face of an angel, twisted by betrayal into something unrecognizable.

"Since forever, old friend," he said in a low voice. "Since forever..."

CHAPTER 12

It wasn't long after Lucifer had dealt with Doug that the bartender came and told him Mara was now available. Lucifer picked up his tequila sunrise with one hand and beckoned Belial to follow with his other, and the two went up the staircases to the sixth floor of Lust.

The two demons who stood guard outside Mara's office at first showed deference to Lucifer, but once they spotted Belial, they became like cats on edge. Eyes narrowed, shoulders stiffened, and lips tightened. Lucifer cast a glance in his ally's direction. Belial wore a slight grin on his face.

Belial had earned his reputation as one of the fiercest torturers in all of Hell through eons of effort and dedication to his craft. These two either knew him by reputation, or they'd been former subjects of his.

"Let us through, boys," said Lucifer. "Belial is with me."

"You heard the boss," said Belial, staring at each of them. His gaze remained fixed, but theirs faltered and they allowed their eyes to fall.

"Mara is expecting you, sire," said one of them.

Lucifer nodded to him and then walked up to the door. He pushed it open and stepped inside the office. Mara lay spread out on the couch, wearing a pair of red leather pants and a tight shirt that matched. Just as she was about to stand, Lucifer stopped her with a gesture.

"It's all right, Mara. You look quite comfortable there."

Mara remained on the couch and Lucifer moved around and settled into the chair. Belial came and stood by his side, acting as a sentry. Mara's gaze fell on the demon, and though she kept trying to look at Lucifer, the Morningstar noticed how her eyes always seemed to drift back to Belial. Just like the two outside, Lucifer wasn't sure if Mara's apprehension came from Belial's reputation or her own experiences.

"Is there something I can help you with, my Lord?" she asked.

"Yes, you can cut out that royal talk." Lucifer jerked a thumb in Belial's direction. "I get enough of it from this one. Could do with a bit of a respite."

"I understand, my lie—Lucifer." Mara corrected herself and now sat upright. Despite Lucifer's command that she make herself comfortable, it was clear that would be impossible while in their presence. Could have been because of Lucifer alone, because of Belial, or the combination of the two.

"Belial has arrived from Hell to tell me a very unpleasant story," said Lucifer. "Apparently, there have been a number of prisoners who escaped from Cocytus."

"How's that possible?" asked Mara.

"Your mistress did it once," said Lucifer. "Or have you forgotten?"

He referred to Lilith, the first human corrupted by Hell and transformed into a demon. She was also the reason Cocytus was forged in the first place, as a way to appease Heaven after she created the first cambions, who later evolved along different branches into the monsters that populated the Earth. Vampires, werewolves, skinwalkers, incubi and succubi, and many more all the result of Lilith.

"No, I have not," said Mara. "Though I wouldn't mention that around her. It tends to be something of a sore subject."

Lucifer looked down at his drink before taking a slow sip. "I'm aware." There was a pang that ran through his body. Yet another regret in the long list. He'd been so desperate to prevent another war that he happily threw Lilith to the wolves. Even though the only crime she'd been guilty of was enjoying the same freedom he himself had fought for.

It was *not* his proudest moment. But that could be said of many actions he'd taken since The Fall.

"Let's leave what was done to Lilith in the past for the time being," he said. "I need to focus on the problem at hand. Lilith escaped, but she did so in order to claim something she had right to. And it all worked out in the end. She has her seat on the Infernal Court, and Cross' involvement is what led to me being here."

"But you don't foresee such an amicable resolution with these escapees," said Mara.

Lucifer shook his head. "We are talking about the most vile souls to have ever crossed through the Gates of Hell. And them being on Earth doesn't bode well for anyone. They pose a greater threat to humanity than any run-of-the-mill demon, and that could push Heaven to take more drastic action against our kind."

"'*Our*' kind." Mara said it almost with a scoff. And by the widening of her eyes, it was clear she realized her mistake right away.

But just as she opened her mouth—presumably to apologize—Belial was already right in front of her. His hand wrapped around her throat and plucked her off the couch, then he turned and threw her.

Mara struck the glass overlooking the club. It was still intact, though Belial seemed intent to do otherwise. Before Mara could pull herself back together, Belial grabbed her again and slammed her against the glass. Now, cracks began to form in a weblike pattern beneath the point of impact.

"You *dare* speak that way to the Morningstar? To our liberator? I should drag your soul back to Hell myself and see how many times I can break you!"

"Belial!"

Lucifer's voice bounced around the room, deepening to an unnatural octave. His eyes flared yellow and wings began to emerge from his back. Lucifer could feel the hellfire burning within his body, screaming for a release. But rather than unleash it upon Belial, he took a deep breath and tried to maintain his cool. His eyes dimmed, but the wings remained unfurled.

Belial seemed to understand just how serious the Morningstar was. He pulled Mara away from the window and allowed her to stand on her own two feet. She had fire in her own eyes, but she contained it and refused to look at Lucifer.

"I apologize, Morningstar," she said. "I didn't mean that. It just slipped out."

"You have a point." Lucifer flexed his wings to emphasize his words. "More than any of The Fallen, I still bear the vestiges of Heaven. A reminder of everything I gave up when I rebelled."

"*Some* of us still remember just how much you gave up

for our freedom," said Belial, casting a side-glance in Mara's direction.

"Enough, Belial. We have more important things to concern ourselves with. Namely these escapees from Cocytus. They have to be contained and in order to do that, I need help."

"What can I do?" asked Mara.

"Every soul that enters Cocytus is branded. With the aid of dark magic, I can get a sense of where the closest soul is. And I know of one man in Chicago who commands the darkest magic of all."

"You're talking about Odysseus Black."

Lucifer confirmed with a nod.

"Who is Odysseus Black?" asked Belial.

"Powerful sorcerer around these parts. Uses magic to extend his lifespan. He's been around for centuries," said Mara. "Though I think you might be barking up the wrong tree with him."

"And why's that?" asked Lucifer.

"Lilith had some dealings with Black during the period she was running Lust. She told me that he got the shit kicked out of him by Cross' witch buddy, but to keep an eye out for his antics."

"And have there been any antics?"

Mara shook her head. "He's been quiet. I haven't even heard his name mentioned in months."

"Where can I find him?"

"Assuming he hasn't skipped town?" asked Mara. "He usually holes up in a dive bar in Englewood. I can write down the address for you."

"That would be helpful," said Lucifer. "We can drop in and see if he's up for accepting visitors."

"Given the silence from his camp lately, I'd say that's a big fat no," said Mara. "But I'm pretty sure he'd make an exception for the Prince of Darkness."

Lucifer couldn't help cringing at that moniker. It was the complete antithesis of what he was meant for—to be a bringer of knowledge, truth, and light. As much as he wanted to hoist all the blame on the Divine Choir for their role in his branding, by hiding away in his tower and refusing to fight, he'd accepted their judgment and labels.

"I believe that concludes our business then." Lucifer reached into his jacket and drew a phone. He passed it to Mara. "If you could just type in the address, we'll be on our way."

Mara accepted the phone and preceded to enter the location of Black's bar. But as she did, she paused. Lucifer studied her face as she seemed to freeze, just staring at the phone.

"Mara? Is everything all right?"

Mara shook her head, like snapping out of a trance. "Sorry. I just remembered something." She met Lucifer's gaze. "These demons, do you think any of them would be here? In the city, I mean."

Lucifer looked to Belial for an answer. The demon cleared his throat before speaking.

"Of course it's possible, but I don't think it'd be likely. The Morningstar's presence is a unique one and any demon within the city limits could sense it."

"You think they'd try to avoid the city so they wouldn't risk running into him?" asked Mara.

"If you escaped from prison, would you want to be in the same vicinity as your jailer?" asked Belial.

"That depends," said Mara. "Am I more interested in survival or revenge?"

Lucifer rubbed his chin in thought. Naturally most would stick to evasion and avoid being captured and sent back. But there were also those who would no doubt want some form of retribution to make up for the time they spent imprisoned.

"You know something, don't you?" asked Lucifer.

"Maybe, maybe not," said Mara. "It could just be a coincidence."

"I don't believe in coincidences," said Lucifer. "Tell me what you know."

Mara sighed. "A cop came to me earlier. Asking for information about a killer that might be possessed by a demon. Seems a priest was murdered in a pretty brutal fashion. And he left a message. A reference to a passage from *Paradise Lost*."

"What passage?"

"'Better to reign in Hell then serve in Heav'n.'"

"Feels fairly thin," said Belial.

"He's right, religious overtones aren't exactly unheard of when it comes to serial killers," said Mara. "But the guy's been around the supernatural scene. He's a friend of Cross, actually. Well…kind of. They didn't seem all that close when Cross introduced me to him."

"Might be worth a look after we speak with Odysseus," said Lucifer. "Who is this officer?"

"He's a detective," said Mara. "Hold on."

She got up from the couch and went through a door that led to a staircase up to the apartment above. While she was gone, Lucifer finished his drink and went to the bar. He examined the selection and poured himself a glass of scotch.

"You don't really think one of those demons would be stupid enough to challenge you, do you?" asked Belial.

"It's a possibility, and one we might as well entertain," said Lucifer, sipping the drink. "If this is one of my prisoners trying to get my attention, then ignoring the problem will just mean he steps up the murders. No, I have to look into it. And besides, it's not like I've got a bevy of leads to begin with."

"I don't like the idea of some sort of meandering chase, and it feels like that's what we're about to embark on."

"It's like I told you before, old friend—you don't *have* to be here. If you choose to return to Hell, I won't hold it against you."

"No," said Belial. "I gave you my word and I stand by it."

Mara returned from upstairs and held out her arm. In her hand was a business card. Lucifer accepted it and read the name imprinted on the face.

"Detective Wayne Cooper," he said. "Thank you, my dear. With any luck, he may have something that can help us in our search."

"Just be careful," said Mara. "Both with Black and this demon. Neither sound like something I'd want to get mixed up with."

"I'll keep that in mind." He finished the drink and set the empty glass on the bar. "Come, Belial. We've got a date with a sorcerer."

CHAPTER 13

Englewood was regarded as one of Chicago's most-dangerous neighborhoods. Vacant homes and lots dotted the landscape in various states of disrepair. Some were boarded up, others didn't even bother and they'd become a haven for the city's homeless populations.

Lucifer could sense the dark energy in this neighborhood. It had a troubled history, dating all the way back to the late 1800s when America's first serial killer, H.H. Holmes, had converted an old hotel into his infamous "murder castle." The despair and horror lingered in the air, and that energy could be used to fuel all manner of black magic.

It was little wonder why Odysseus Black had chosen this place as his base of operations.

The bar Mara had directed Lucifer and Belial to was a one-story building that had seen better days. There was no visible entrance on the first story, but stairs led down to a basement access door.

"This is definitely it," said Lucifer. "If Black is indeed hiding out here, he's doing a good job of it. I can't sense any unnatural magical energy."

Lucifer approached the stairs, but when he tried to

step down on the first one, he found he couldn't. He tried again, but once more something was blocking him. There was some kind of invisible barrier that prevented him from venturing any further.

"Sire?" asked Belial.

Lucifer grunted. "How many times must we go over this, Belial?"

"I'm sorry. But what seems to be the problem?"

"The problem is our friend seems quite paranoid," said Lucifer. "There's some sort of warding magic, I can't get through."

"May I?"

Lucifer sighed and stepped away from the stairs. He leaned against the side of the building. "You can try, but I don't see what the use is. If the wards are powerful enough to keep out me, then certainly they're powerful enough to—"

The sound of banging on metal cut off Lucifer's train of thought. He looked over and was surprised to see Belial had managed to descend the steps and was now slamming his fist against the metal door. He had a dazed look as he cocked his head to the side..

"What the fuck…?" he muttered under his breath.

It didn't make any sense. How could the wards have prevented him from entering, but been useless against Belial? Lucifer knew his powers had been weakened eons ago by the creation of Cocytus, but just how weak had he become? Was it possible that he was now little more than some common demon?

Belial grunted and slammed both his palms against the door. He glanced back at Lucifer. "There's no answer."

"This place is a shithole. There's no reason anyone

would go to the trouble of using magic to lock it up unless there was something worth hiding past that door," said Lucifer. "Break it down."

Belial grinned. Lucifer could tell he was going to enjoy the opportunity to dish out some violence. Even if it was just against an inanimate object for now, the warding meant the potential for some action on the other side. Belial raised his leg and kicked the door in. It blew off its hinges and flew inside.

That had broken whatever warding magic was on it and now Lucifer found he was able to move down the steps. Belial stepped aside and allowed him to go in first.

There was a stench of death lingering in the air. Lucifer entered what was a very dingy dive bar. A few bodies were piled up in one corner and judging from the smell, they'd been there for some time.

A sound came from behind the bar. Lucifer turned his attention and saw a trio of beasts rising up, covered in blood-stained fur. They growled as crimson eyes fixated on the new arrivals.

"Lycans," spat Belial. "Lilith's bastard offspring. We should have eliminated the lot of them when they first started to appear."

The werewolves apparently didn't like Belial's disdain as their growls only grew in intensity.

"I think you hurt their feelings, Belial," said Lucifer.

One of them jumped on the counter and slowly moved closer on all fours. His lips curled back from his teeth, drool beginning to drip from the edges of his mouth. He pounced, hands out and claws extended as he flew towards Belial.

But the archdemon wouldn't be taken so easily. Belial

grabbed the lycan in mid-air and flipped him around, slamming him against the wall. Without wasting another second, Belial grabbed the lycan's head and twisted. A yelp escaped the wolf's lips just prior to a loud *crack*. But Belial continued twisting until he pulled the head clean off. He turned towards the other lycans and held up the head for them to see.

"If that's the best you can do, then I'm afraid I'm sorely disappointed," he said before tossing the head at them.

It landed on the counter and rolled towards the other two. The remaining lycans examined the head of their fallen brother, their crimson eyes pulsating as their hair began to rise and their ears pinned to the sides of their heads. One of them started to bark. Belial cracked his knuckles and gave a snicker.

But then, Lucifer came between the demon and the werewolves, holding up his palms to both sides. "Perhaps we can try a different tactic." Then he said to the lycans, "We're not here to fight. We came to speak to your master."

"He *killed* our brother!" shouted one of the lycans.

"Your brother made the first move," said Lucifer.

"You broke down the door."

"Because you wouldn't answer," said Lucifer. "If you had, maybe this could have gone very differently. Now if you want to end up losing your head like your idiot brother, I'm quite certain my friend would be more than happy to accommodate you."

"Ecstatic, in fact," said Belial. "I'm curious to see just how many bones I'd have to break before I could shove his head up his own ass."

"You see? He's more than willing to keep fighting. And as you've already seen, it's a fight you're unlikely to win," said Lucifer. "Option B: we behave like civilized monsters and you tell Odysseus Black that the Morningstar is here to speak with him."

The jaws of both beasts slackened. They exchanged glances between each other and then both looked at Lucifer in unison. Slowly their forms started to shift, from wolves back to men. But the same expression of disbelief remained, as if it were frozen on their faces.

"Did…did you just say the Morningstar?"

"I'm not one for stuttering, so I believe you heard me quite clearly the first time," said Lucifer. "Now go. Inform your boss that the Devil has dropped by for a chat."

One of them slinked away and went to a closed door. He knocked a few times and after there was no answer, he opened it and stepped inside. Lucifer couldn't hear the conversation on the other side of the door, but it probably didn't matter if he could anyway. After a few minutes, the man emerged again and held the door open.

"He said he'll see you."

"Thank you."

Lucifer walked towards the doorway and went through. But just as Belial was about to go in, the lycan blocked his path, changing back to his wolf form as he did. Belial grabbed the lycan by the throat and the lycan in turn grabbed Belial as well. Lucifer turned back and sighed.

"I thought we'd already been through this."

"Boss said just you. No entourage," said the lycan.

"Belial, play nice while I'm in the meeting."

"You can't expect me to let you go in alone!"

"On the contrary, that's *precisely* what I expect of you," said Lucifer. "Now please, do as I wish. We're in Mr. Black's house, it's only polite we abide by the rules he's set."

Belial let out a low growl, but released his grip. The lycan did the same. Belial folded his arms across his chest and stared at the lycan. "You'd better have something worth drinking if I'm stuck smelling dog hair."

The lycan shifted back to human form and went towards the bar. "Follow me."

"There, that's the spirit," said Lucifer before closing the door behind him.

He stepped deeper into the room and glanced around. It was a massive office with bookshelves lining the walls. But he was the only one inside. As he scanned the room, he saw an open passage with stone steps leading deep underground.

"I do hope you're not wasting my time, Odysseus..." muttered the Morningstar as he began his descent.

The steps spiraled down and when Lucifer reached the bottom, he saw that the light was dim down here. There was also a stench. Not of death like around the lycans, but more despair. Mixed with the unmistakable stink of a man who hadn't bathed in days, if not longer.

"So...look who's here."

The words were slurred. Lucifer looked towards it and saw a figure stumbling from the shadows. His crimson suit was wrinkled with the shirt unbuttoned completely, revealing his gut hanging over his loosened belt. In one hand was a bottle of malt liquor, the other holding a cigar.

"The great Odysseus Black," said Lucifer. "I'll admit, you don't exactly live up to your reputation."

Odysseus gave a chuckle that was punctuated by a hiccup. "Yer a funny one, Mr. Scratch. So why you here anyway? This the part where my soul gets dragged to Hell?"

"That's not my department, actually," said Lucifer.

"Besides, I'm retired."

Odysseus chortled. "Who you bullshittin'? Nobody never heard of no Satan retiring."

"Well, things change."

"Whatever, man."

"You seem a bit despondent, Odysseus," said Lucifer. "Hiding down here, trying to drink yourself to death, warding your place against intruders."

"Yeah, well. 'Least it's jes' you an' not some halo-wearin' fuck."

"Angels?" said Lucifer. "You're trying to hide from angels?"

"No shit, Sherlock. They not exactly my biggest fans. Not since that punk Pyriel gave me that book. So, I'm stayin' off their radar."

"So your wards...they were only to keep angels out?"

"Yeah, so? What would you do if you had those Big Bird bastards on your tail?"

That was why Belial was able to enter. It didn't explain why Lucifer was blocked. Or maybe it did, and the truth of that was something he didn't want to acknowledge for the moment.

"Let's focus on why *I'm* here for the moment," said Lucifer. "I'm here to ask a favor. There are some souls on Earth that are tied to mine. I could use your magicks to get a sense of where they might be."

Odysseus guzzled down what was left of the bottle and tossed it over his shoulder. "An' why should I help you?" He turned away and waddled towards a corner of the room where a mini-fridge sat. When he opened the door, Lucifer could see rows of malt liquor. Odysseus took one and popped the cap off.

"I heard you suffered a defeat recently. That plus your fear of the angels has driven you to hide yourself away," said Lucifer.

"What's it to ya?"

"As you're well aware, I have something of a reputation in the world," said Lucifer. "Tell me, if you had the Morningstar in your corner, just what do you think that would do for your reputation around these parts?"

Odysseus took a swig from the bottle while staring at Lucifer. "You talkin' a deal with the Devil. Memory serves, that's got one'a them...whatchacallit...monkey's paw qualities to it, right?"

"That's the theory. And if you were dealing with any other demon, I'd say you should tread very carefully." Lucifer slid his hands into his pants pockets. "But I think you know I'm far beyond any simple demon. And I'm a man who keeps my word."

"So why they call you the Prince of Lies then?"

Lucifer rolled his eyes. "Propaganda, nothing more. I assure you, Mr. Black, I *always* keep my promises. Not once have I ever broken a single one."

"So why you need me to work some mojo for you anyway?" asked Odysseus. "Why can't you do it yourself?"

"Did I say I couldn't do it myself?" asked Lucifer. He really couldn't, but there was no reason Odysseus had to know that little fact. "Your assistance would be very valuable in this regard. And if you provide me with the help I need, then I'd be happy to put in a good word for you with anyone else I may come across. Including the new manager of Lust."

Odysseus cocked an eyebrow. "Lust?"

Lucifer nodded. "You haven't had a chance to get acquainted with her. But as I understand, at one point you were quite connected to the club when Asmodeus was in charge. I could see to it that you get back on your feet."

"What about the witch?"

"Ah yes, I heard about your little...spat with Tessa Kang," said Lucifer. "Provided you stick to your lane and don't attempt to try anything bigger—such as coordinating with rogue angels—I doubt she'd have reason to even notice you."

Odysseus guzzled down more of the bottle. He let out a belch and then said, "Okay, I'll help you out. Tell me what I gotta do."

A deal had been struck and now Lucifer was one step closer to learning just where the escaped prisoners had gone to. However, there was something else gnawing at him. Black's warding magicks had been designed to keep out angels. All of The Fallen were supposed to have been so corrupted by Hell that they'd been transformed into demons.

Lucifer had always believed he himself was transformed, too, and his wings were just cosmetic. But it seemed he was wrong. Even though he could command hellfire and his eyes bore the markings of the pit, part of him was still an angel.

He was neither one nor the other. Instead, he was something else.

CHAPTER 14

While Odysseus began preparing for the spell, Lucifer took the opportunity to go check on Belial. He wondered just how his self-appointed bodyguard had been doing with the lycans. After all, he *had* killed one of their number, so it was likely they weren't too fond of him. And he'd made his distaste for them quite clear as well.

Before he stepped through the door leading back to the bar, Lucifer prepared himself for what might be waiting on the other side. Would they be sniping at each other? Would Belial have killed the remaining two? A multitude of gruesome scenarios played out in the thoughts of the Morningstar, but nothing could have prepared him for what he found when he opened the door.

There were indeed raised voices, but not in anger. Instead, laughter echoed in the small bar. Belial and the two lycans sat at the counter and passed a bottle of rum between them, refilling each other's glasses, telling jokes, and laughing together.

One of the lycans looked away from the circle and caught sight of Lucifer. He nudged Belial with his elbow and said, "Hey B, looks like your boss wants you back on the clock."

"Ah, he's so much more than a boss," said Belial, his speech slurring just a bit. "The Morningstar saved us all from the tyrannical rule of Heaven! Freed us from the yoke of slavery! Everyone, a toast to the Lightbringer!"

"Cheers!" the two lycans said in unison just before all three hit their glasses together.

Lucifer came up behind Belial and placed a hand on his shoulder. Belial looked up at him with a smile plastered over his face. He sluggishly reached a hand and placed it on Lucifer's shoulder as well. Lucifer looked past the three and saw several empty bottles lying on the counter.

"Not so easy for the likes of us to get drunk," he said. "Just how much have the three of you had?"

"We lost count somewhere in the early double-digits," said one of the lycans, punctuated by a hiccup and then a snicker.

"How'd it go downstairs with Yodyssus…Yodeesys… Yo—" Belial's chortled as his attempts to pronounce the name turned to laughter. "Y'know, the magic man."

"Odysseus," said Lucifer, a smile tugging at the corner of his lips. "He's preparing the spell right now. Soon we'll be able to get a sense of where these demons are located."

"You need me t' stand guard? Make sure he doesn't **hic** try no funny business?"

"I've got a feeling I can manage just fine on my own," said Lucifer. "Perhaps you should stay here with your friends."

"Frenz?" asked Belial, then swung his arm around to presumably point at the lycans. But he just kind of flailed about instead. "Nah, nah, I'd never be frenz wit' half-breeds like these mongrels!"

"Yeah, fuck you too, Hellspawn."

"Hey!" Belial grabbed the lycan by his fur and pulled his face close. "Thas...*Heaven*spawn!"

The three of them laughed and Belial picked up the bottle to refill everyone's glass. He held the bottle out to Lucifer. "You wanna join us for a drink, milord?" Belial chuckled and then added, "Sorry, you don' like that kinda stuff. I forget."

"It's fine, my friend," said Lucifer. "You...keep watch over these two while Odysseus and I complete the spell."

"You betcha!" Belial looked back at the lycans. "Y'hear that? No funny stuff! I got my eye on you!"

The laughter followed Lucifer as he returned to Odysseus' office and then back down the stairway located in the hidden passage. At the foot of the stairs, he saw Odysseus drawing a sigil on the floor. Two concentric circles and inside was a character that seemed to be made up of a few Latin phrases crammed together.

"It seems I'm the only one not drunk," said Lucifer. "I'm beginning to feel left out."

"There's plenty of booze in the fridge if you want," said Odysseus. "'Sides, I whipped up a little detox spell to sober me up for this."

"You should try bottling it, you'd make a fortune." Lucifer took off his suit jacket and carefully draped it over the back of a chair.

Odysseus gave a chuckle. "If only. But magic's not that simple." He rose to his feet and examined the red paint to check his work. "Okay, think that about does it. You ready for this?"

Lucifer rolled up the sleeves of his black silk shirt. "Absolutely. The sooner I can find these demons, the sooner I can get back to enjoying my retirement."

"This is a kinda variation on a soul mate locator spell," said Odysseus. "Way I figure, if these souls are linked to your power, then it's not all that dissimilar from a soul mate."

"Interesting interpretation. Certainly gives a new definition for soul mates."

"Sit in the center of the circle."

Lucifer stepped inside the sigil and sat down, folding his legs in front of him. Odysseus took a rolled-up map from the table and unfurled it in front of Lucifer. It was a map of the world. He went over to the table and took a knife and a cup, holding them both out to Lucifer.

"Need you to cut your hand an' bleed into the cup," said Odysseus. "Once the spell's in progress, I'll pour the blood over the map an' it'll move to the locations where those demons are."

"Very well." Lucifer set the cup down in front of him on top of the map. He pressed the blade against his palm and drew it in a downward motion. With his fist closed, he held his hand over the cup and squeezed, allowing the blood to drip down into the cup.

"That should be enough." Odysseus sat across from Lucifer, then took the cup and moved it to the side.

Lucier set the knife down and clasped his hands together. A soft, warm light appeared in the gaps between his fingers. When the light dissipated, he separated his hands and the wound was completely healed.

"Close your eyes and focus on something connected to those souls," said Odysseus.

Lucifer took a deep breath as he lowered his eyelids. His

memory went back to the day when he created Cocytus. He remembered all the power he had put into constructing this prison in one portion of Hell, disconnected from everything else. A place of absolute despair, where those imprisoned would have no contact with any other being from now until the end of time.

The power that had gone into its creation was immense. It was difficult to quantify the amount of time it had taken given how differently it moved in Hell. But it was the equivalent of running a marathon that lasted for months. By the time Lucifer had completed construction, he was almost too weak to make it back to his tower.

He remembered arriving on the front steps and collapsing on them. It took every ounce of his remaining strength just to crawl up the stairs and past the front door. Once there, Lucifer had passed out, and he stayed that way for some time before waking again.

And when he had woken, that was when he realized for the first time just how much of his power Cocytus had required. His reserves were utterly depleted and he felt as weak as a newborn kitten. The self-imposed isolation became all-consuming from that point on. Lucifer almost never held sessions of the Infernal Court unless it was a matter of urgency or importance. He was afraid the others would sense his diminished standing and that he would be challenged for rule.

Then the challenge had come in the form of Abraxas. One of his lieutenants in the rebellion. Abraxas knew what the others had failed to sense—that the Morningstar no longer commanded the same power as before. Fortunately, nobody had ever really trusted Abraxas since even before The Fall, and it was easy enough to rally the support necessary to stop him once and for all.

The memories merged together and suddenly, Lucifer saw something else. He opened his eyes, but he was no longer in Odysseus' basement. The eyes he was looking through were not his own. He looked up and saw a crucifix with a shape in the form of the Nazarene hanging from it. The setting sun provided a backlight for the scene, making it difficult to make out the man's features. And it took a moment before Lucifer realized that he wasn't looking at a wooden reproduction, but this was a memory of the *actual* Crucifixion.

The scene changed and now he was in a desolate area. The hot sun beat down upon him, but he felt no effects of the heat. The terrain was barren and rocky, without any sign of civilization in sight. And up ahead, he saw the Nazarene again. This time, his head was bowed in prayer and his lips cracked and dry from thirst.

The being whose eyes Lucifer stared through approached the Nazarene and held out a stone. It shifted and changed, becoming a loaf of bread, and this he offered to the starving man.

"All you have to do is join us," said the being. "You need not be a slave to the whims of Heaven. Whatever they've told you is a lie."

The Nazarene didn't say a word. And Lucifer could feel the anger growing. He knew now it was a demon whose eyes he was looking through. A demon who tried to convince the Nazarene to turn against the angels. And yet, the demon had failed every single attempt at temptation.

"Yes, I remember you now…" muttered Lucifer, though even he couldn't hear the words as he spoke them. He was still locked in the memories.

The world changed again and Lucifer now stood in a church. The image of the Nazarene on the crucifix was emblazoned all around him. And the demon began work on one of his targets, carving into the flesh of a man of the cloth.

The priest's screams sent waves of ecstasy through the demon. He took his time carving into the priest's flesh, savoring every moment of the experience. And when the priest had finally had enough and the life faded from his eyes, the demon dipped his fingers in the priest's blood. He drew the numbers on the back of the confessional booth. The reference to *Paradise Lost* that Mara had told Lucifer about.

The image suddenly retreated from Lucifer's gaze as if he were being yanked away. He snapped back to the present and found himself staring into the face of Odysseus Black.

Lucifer gasped at the sudden transition and took a few breaths. He gave a sigh and relaxed his body, then finally spoke. "I could see through his eyes."

"'His'?" asked Odysseus. "You mean as in only one? Thought you said there was a whole mess of demons that escaped."

"I did, but it was just the one I could connect to," said Lucifer. "No doubt because he's the closest. Perhaps even the strongest."

"That don't make sense," said Odysseus. "Look at the map."

Lucifer did and he saw that Odysseus had poured his blood onto it as he said he would. But the blood hadn't moved at all. It just remained on the map in one large blob.

"What is this?"

"The spell didn't work," said Odysseus.

"I can *see* that." Lucifer's heart quickened and he shifted his eyes from the map to Odysseus. His tone sharpened when he asked, "*Why?*"

"No idea. Not like we're dealin' wi—"

Lucifer grabbed Odysseus throat. He held out his free hand and hellfire began to form in his palm, taking the shape of a dagger. Lucifer's yellow eyes burned like hot coals and he brought the flaming dagger towards Odysseus' face.

"You wouldn't try to play any games with me, would you, sorcerer?"

"N-no!" pleaded Odysseus. "Look, man, I *did* what you asked! We dealin' with some very unusual magic here, the kind of stuff there ain't no rulebook for!"

Lucifer considered the sorcerer's words and had to conclude there was truth in them. As the warding spell had proven, Lucifer was unique—not quite demon, but also not quite angel. And as far as Lucifer knew, no other celestial had ever attempted to single-handedly create a construct like Cocytus. This was certainly uncharted territory.

He released his grip on Odysseus and the hellfire dagger vanished. Lucifer stood and began ascending the steps. At the very least, he knew Mara's theory was correct—the man who killed that priest was indeed possessed by one of the demons from Cocytus. And Lucifer knew exactly which demon he was dealing with.

"So...our deal still good?" Odysseus' voice echoed up the stairwell. "You gonna put in that word for me?"

CHAPTER 15

Wayne Cooper had seen some gruesome sights in his career as a Chicago police officer, as well as some unbelievable sights. But what he looked at now was certainly a new one for him. Inside the St. Procopious Catholic Church in the neighborhood of Pilsen, he stared into the dead eyes of the victim. Or at least he would have been if there were any eyes left. As it stood, they'd been removed, replaced by two coins. And the victim's head relieved from his body and set upon a silver platter.

"Jesus...."

Wayne stood and turned to face Janice as she approached. Her eyes were fixed on the severed head and she covered her mouth, as if she was about to vomit. She seemed capable of restraining it just to a gag, though.

"Don't really figure him for a suspect," said Wayne. "What with the whole crucifixion thing and all."

"Aren't you the comedian," she said with a roll of her eyes.

Wayne smirked just for an instant and then became business again. "Got anything for me?"

She sighed and flipped through her small notebook. "John Dawson, he was a priest here."

"So the pattern continues," said Wayne. "We have any religious references this time?"

"M.14:8-11," said Janice. "And I can save you some time, I did a search for it on my phone. Came up with a Bible passage."

"What's it say?"

Janice took out her phone and brought up the passage again. "'Prompted by her mother, she said, "Give me the head of John the Baptist here on a platter." The king was grieved, yet out of regard for his oaths and for the guests, he commanded it to be given; he sent and had John beheaded in the prison. The head was brought on a platter and given to the girl, who brought it to her mother.'"

"So now, a priest named John gets his head lopped off and left for us literally on a silver platter." Wayne rubbed his eyes. He started to develop that familiar hatred of the job that came with cases like this. "Is there anything else we know?"

"It's pretty much the same as the last guy," said Janice. "Murder happened after-hours, body was discovered in the morning. Nobody seen going in or out."

"Yeah, well get forensics in here. Maybe the guy slipped up, left something behind."

"You really believe that?" asked Janice.

Wayne moved away from the body and walked past Janice down the center aisle. "Of course not. But what choice do we have? No witnesses, no cameras, nothing."

He left the chapel and out the front doors. It was afternoon now and he took a seat on the curb. Times like this, he wished he hadn't quit smoking. Wayne fumbled through his pockets hoping for some gum or a hard candy or something he could focus his oral fixation on. But he had nothing.

"Hey, Coop."

He didn't even turn to look at Janice, just linked his hands together and breathed in the air. "Don't suppose you smoke?"

"No, why?"

"Forget it. What is it, Wagner?"

"Seems you were right, this is looking like a serial." Janice sat down on the steps beside him. "So do you want to fill me in on that tip you went to check out the other day?"

He hadn't told her about his conversation with Mara, not in any sort of depth at least. And in truth, he wasn't sure if he should. Janice was interested in learning more about the unusual aspects of crime in this city, but once that particular door was opened, it would never be closed again. Wayne Cooper was living proof of that.

"Just what I told you, I found out what those numbers meant," he said. "Definitely some religious whackjob we're dealing with here."

"What's the next step?"

"Forensics will check the scene, let us know if they find anything."

"But you don't think they will."

Wayne shook his head. "The guy's pretty methodical. You saw both bodies. The cuts were clean and precise. That kind of thing takes time and effort. This bastard knows what he's doing, he knows how to keep his cool, and he knows how long it will take."

"And there's something else, isn't there? I can tell you're holding back on me."

"Don't know what you're talking about."

"Alexandra Hughes?"

Wayne's blood froze when he heard that. But it thawed quickly, melting with the heat of a rising anger. "Where did you hear that name?"

"I was looking through some of your old cases," said Janice. "Killed her children while they slept. But there seemed to be some holes in the report and you said you had some assistance from Luther Cross."

Those holes were there for a reason. Alexandra Hughes had been possessed by a demon when she killed her children. It was one of the first cases Wayne had worked on with Luther Cross, and when he fully came to accept just how very real the supernatural was.

It was also a case doomed to fail. Despite Luther's best efforts, Hughes didn't survive the exorcism. In his report, Wayne had to write up the cause of death as unknown. Nobody questioned him about it. Enough people in the department knew there were things that couldn't—or *shouldn't*—be explained.

"What's your point?"

"This is the same Cross who I met, right? The one people whisper about in the department," she said. "So if we're dealing with something weird, then shouldn't we go find him?"

"You can't, he's not around anymore," said Wayne. "You're just going to have to trust me when I tell you that you don't want to get involved in this shit."

"I'm a big girl, Coop. How about you let me make those kinds of decisions for myself?"

Wayne sighed and stood from the curb. He jerked his head and turned west. "There's a bakery just around the corner and I need some coffee."

Wayne crossed the street with Janice following. At the next street, he took a right and tucked away was the small bakery. He didn't give much time for Janice to catch up, just walked right up to the counter and looked over the selection of artisanal coffees they had on display.

"What can I get you?" asked the guy behind the counter, wearing an apron and a beanie cap.

"Coffee, black. To go," said Wayne.

"What kind of coffee? We've got—"

"Surprise me, kid. I just need caffeine, don't give a damn how it tastes."

By the time the barista began preparing Wayne's order, Janice had caught up to him. Wayne took the coffee and paid in cash, then left the shop. He crossed the street, but away from the church. Janice ran up by his side.

"You wanna tell me where you're going now?"

"There's a small park just down this street. I'm going to sit and drink my coffee and think."

"What about me?"

"Join me if you like or go back to the crime scene."

They entered Throop Park, with a basketball court on one side and a playground on the other. It was a school day and still early at that, so the park was empty. Wayne sat on a bench facing the playground and began to sip his coffee through the hole in the plastic lid.

"I'm really not in the mood for games here, Coop. So if you want to piss around, then maybe—"

"Shut up," said Wayne. "You've been asking a lot of questions lately and I suppose you could say I'm ready to answer them."

"Okay, great," said Janice. "That's all I want. So where do we sta—"

"First thing's first." He looked at her, his piercing eyes gazing hard into hers. Almost as if he were warning her. "I want to give you a choice."

"A choice? I don't think I follow…"

"When I learned about this stuff, I didn't have a choice. I was sort of dragged into it, you know. Kicking and screaming. And now as I look back all these years later, I wish to God someone had given *me* the option of continuing to live in ignorance. Because if I tell you, then you'll have to live with it for the rest of your life. And it's not an easy burden to bear.

"So, I'm giving you the choice I never had. The choice to go about your life, solving crimes you can make sense of, and leaving the fucked-up ones like this to the people who are already damned."

"I said I wanted to know," said Janice. "I haven't changed my mind about that."

"That's because you haven't really given it the proper thought," said Wayne. "What I've learned in the past ten years is that there's a lot more weird in this world than I'd been led to believe. And it's not a simple kind of weird. This is beyond basic concepts of good and evil. The complexities alone were almost enough to drive me to the nuthouse."

Janice slowly exhaled, the breath audible as it passed her lips. "You wanna talk complex, Coop? You just said you'd tell me, and now you're still dancing around the issue. So why don't you just sack up and spit it out?"

Wayne looked away while raising the cup to his lips for another sip. The coffee was warm and bitter. He stared at the plastic lid, watching the steam flow from the hole. And then he said, "No."

Janice threw her arms into the air as she stood. "Oh for fuck's sake..."

"Wait," said Wayne. "What I mean to say is I *will* tell you. But only after you've given it some serious—and I *do* mean *serious*—thought. I want you to contemplate the consequences of knowing too much. Think about every rotten, awful thing you've already been exposed to as a cop. And then multiply it. If you decide that you're ready to hear it, *then* I'll tell you."

"You already know what my answer will be," said Janice.

"Take a few days and dwell on it, then give me your answer."

"Fine," she said. "I'm heading back. You coming or what?"

"I'll be along shortly. Wanna finish my coffee first."

Janice left the park and Wayne watched as she walked down the street before she disappeared behind the houses lining the walk. Was he doing the right thing? Could she really be able to stand learning everything he'd have to tell her about? That choice was hers and whatever she decided, he'd have to keep his promise.

"That was quite an interesting little conversation."

Wayne was startled by the sudden voice breaking through the silence. So much that he nearly spilled his coffee over the front of his shirt, but had somehow manage to narrowly avoid doing so. Wayne stood from the bench on full-alert and turned around.

The man he saw was wearing a white suit with a black shirt. His hair was dark and neatly combed. His features were soft and handsome, but what drew Wayne's eye more than anything else were the bright, yellow eyes.

"You..." muttered Wayne. "I know what you are..."

"Actually, I don't think you really do," he said. "But I know about you, Detective Wayne Cooper. And if you aren't too busy at the moment, I was hoping we might have a little chat."

CHAPTER 16

Lucifer stood calm and relaxed as Wayne Cooper glared at him from across the park. The detective knew all about demons, and so it was no surprise that he'd react negatively to the sight of Lucifer's eyes. But Lucifer felt no need to hide who he really was, so he just calmly approached. In response, Wayne dropped his coffee and reached under his leather jacket.

Lucifer gently held up his hand and spoke in a soothing voice. "Now, now. There's no need for weapons. And besides, you know it wouldn't do any good."

"What do you want? Come back to the scene of the crime so you can gloat?"

"You think I'm your serial-killing demon, but you'd be wrong on that point, my friend. In fact, it's quite the opposite. I'm here to help you."

"'Help'?" asked Wayne. "What is this? Mara didn't want to do me any favors, so she sent you instead?"

"Not quite. Mara *did* tell me about you, but she certainly has no power over me."

Lucifer took a step closer. In response, Wayne stepped back and his arm tightened. Lucifer could tell Wayne had his hand around the holstered gun and was just waiting for an excuse to draw.

"Please, I'd rather not get any blood on this suit," said Lucifer. "Nor do I have any desire to kill you."

"You threatening a cop?"

"Promising, in fact."

"So you'll kill me if I defend myself?"

"No," said Lucifer. "If you open fire upon me, I won't do a thing. Other than roll my eyes at human stupidity and try to find a good dry-cleaner. But my friend, I can't speak for him."

A shadow fell over Wayne. He turned and saw the form of Belial standing behind him. Wayne jumped back and drew the gun. Belial grabbed the barrel and yanked it out of Wayne's hand, then lifted the detective by the shirt collar, hefting him off the ground.

"I think he gets the point, Belial," said Lucifer. "Put him down, I'd rather not cause a scene."

Belial grunted and dropped him. Wayne stumbled when he struck the ground and fell down on his ass. Lucifer moved between Belial and Wayne, then offered a hand. Wayne finally accepted it and allowed Lucifer to help him stand.

"Belial, go fetch Detective Cooper's firearm, thank you," said Lucifer.

"Okay. Mara told you about what happened. So what's that mean? You here to help me or what?" asked Wayne.

"Perhaps we should begin with introductions." The Morningstar held out his hand. "You can call me Lucifer."

Wayne studied the hand held out and then he looked into the yellow eyes of the Devil himself. The color drained from his face and his knees started to weaken to the point that he almost stumbled over again. Wayne braced himself against the park bench to stop from falling.

"You're…the Devil?"

"Never been a fan of that word, but yes. Though I'd really prefer if you just called me by my given name."

Wayne huffed. "Right…I'm sure you would…" He turned away and rubbed his short, blond hair. "Jesus…I'm talking to goddamn Satan himself…"

"Again, just Lucifer is fine. And my companion here is named Belial."

Wayne faced them again and looked at Belial. The taller demon folded his arms, Wayne's gun still in his hand, and uttered a low growl while staring.

"You'll have to excuse him. Not much for manners, I'm afraid. Certainly doesn't help that he's nursing a hangover after drinking with a bunch of werewolves."

"Sure…we've all been there…" said Wayne. "I heard you were in town. Just didn't expect…"

"Mara told me about the dead priest. And the message the killer left. I take it by the police presence over at St. Procopious down the street that there's been another victim."

"That's right. You know anything about it?" asked Wayne.

"You've been a police officer for some time, yes?" asked Lucifer.

"Probably longer than I'd care to admit or remember, sure."

"And in your career, I'm certain you've had to deal with an escaped prisoner or two?"

"Yeah, it happens. Why?"

"Because that's actually what I'm dealing with myself," said Lucifer. "You see, many people think of Hell as a prison, but it's just a place like any other. There are good and bad. However, we *do* have a prison down there and unfortunately, several of the inmates have managed to escape."

"And this guy is one of them?"

"I believe so. Yesterday, I took part in a spell that gave me glimpses of the demon's memories. I saw your priest being butchered through the demon's eyes, in addition to another memory from long ago that confirmed his identity."

"So who are we dealing with then?" asked Wayne.

"His name is Astaroth, and he's fairly dangerous."

"And what did he do that was so bad, he ended up getting thrown in Hell's jail?"

"He tried to tempt…someone."

"That's it?" asked Wayne. "Isn't that kind of what you guys do?"

"This was someone important to the angels. So important that they saw his attempts as a threat upon their very existence," said Lucifer. "And so they wanted an example made of him. I was given a choice—lock him away or they'd deal with it themselves."

"And so you did what they told you to do?"

Lucifer's fingers curled when he heard Wayne's accusation, but he stopped himself from forming them into fists. He took a deep breath. Lucifer could sense Belial's own rage and he held up a hand to stop his friend.

"I wouldn't put it in quite those terms, but yes, that's what happened," said Lucifer. "And now he's back."

"So why the *Paradise Lost* quote?" asked Wayne.

"Astaroth was one of The Fallen, like Belial and the rest of the original demons," said Lucifer. "He believed that in Hell, we could create a better Heaven than the one we rebelled against. So when the angels tried to shape humanity, he intervened on his own cognizance. I'd imagine he sees the murder of these priests as another way of doing just that."

Wayne sat on the bench and scratched his neck. "Okay…but something seems weird. What's any of this got to do with John the Baptist?"

Lucifer cocked an eyebrow. "I'm sorry?"

"The latest victim. His head was chopped off and left on a silver platter. The reference was Matthew something. The part about the head of John the Baptist."

"Interesting…"

"Did Asrototh—"

"Astaroth."

"Whatever. Did…whatshisname have anything to do with John the Baptist?"

"No, he didn't…" said Lucifer, his voice trailing off.

Wayne leaned his head forward, staring at Lucifer's face. "You seem surprised?"

"It's nothing. Perhaps he's just playing games," said Lucifer. "But I'll see if I can find anything useful about this case."

"Maybe you can tell me what kind of demon we're dealing with," said Wayne. "Cross once told me that there are two basic types—there are the ones who need to possess and the ones who can walk around on their own. Which one is he?"

"As one of The Fallen, Astaroth is an archdemon. So presumably he'd have the power to create a form for himself."

"You mean you're not sure?"

"He'd been in Cocytus for centuries, his power could

very well have been weakened to the point that he would need a vessel," said Lucifer. "And of course, archdemons *can* possess humans if they feel like it."

"Though why they'd want to sully themselves by wearing the skin of a talking monkey is a mystery." Those were the first words out of Belial's mouth all morning.

"When we find him, we can ask him." Wayne turned his attention to Lucifer. "Speaking of which, how do we do that? You did your spell thing, so can you use that to find him?"

"Unfortunately no, I wasn't able to track him. And I could only see through his eyes, so I can't give you a description." said Lucifer. "However, I have another ability that I believe can help. Have you ever heard of psychometry?"

"That some kind of psychic thing?"

"A bit, yes," said Lucifer. "By touching something, I can get flashes of where it's been. If you can bring me some artifacts from crime scenes, items the victims were wearing at the time, then we might have a chance of getting a better look at some of this."

"And why would I entertain this?" asked Wayne. "How do I know I can even trust you? You're the Devil."

"You've worked with cambions, witches, and vampires. At one point, did you ever think you could trust such an eccentric cast of characters?"

"Maybe not, but they weren't the goddamn Devil."

"No, no they weren't. But I would think those associations taught you that you can't always believe the hype. Listen, I'd like to give you a chance to think this over."

Lucifer snapped his fingers. There was a quick burst of flame that vanished almost immediately, But in its place and clutched between Lucifer's fingers was a business card of his own. He passed it to Wayne, who accepted the card. On the front it simply said THE MORNINGSTAR with a number and address printed beneath.

"You've already spoken to Mara," said Lucifer.

"Never said I trusted her. She was just the only possible lead I had," said Wayne.

"Very well, but you *do* know some of Cross' friends—Tessa Kang and Alistair Carraway, I believe. I've met them myself. If you contact them, I'm sure they'll put your mind at ease," said Lucifer. "And after you've done your diligence, if you'd like my help, you're free to drop by my home."

"I'll think about it. That's the best I can do right now."

"That's fine. Don't take too much time making your decision, though. We are facing a dangerous threat and the sooner we can put our differences aside, the sooner we can stop Astaroth."

"I should be getting back. Got this nosy partner who's been asking a bunch of questions and don't want her getting suspicious." Wayne looked at Belial and cleared his throat.

"Something wrong, mortal?" asked Belial.

"The gun," said Wayne.

Belial didn't move an inch. Lucifer rolled his eyes.

"Just give him the damn weapon, Belial. We have more important things to concern ourselves with and Detective Cooper is on our side."

"Not sure I'd go *that* far. I'm still playing my cards carefully. This is a fucked-up situation and I've been burned before," said Wayne.

"I understand your concern. And we'll do our best to be accommodating." Lucifer turned his eyes onto Belial. "Won't we?"

Belial grumbled and held out the gun at arm's length,

then dropped it. That action caused Wayne to flinch. He gave the demon an angry glare as he bent down to retrieve his weapon.

"Easy with that," said Wayne. "Damn thing could've gone off."

"Ask if I care," said Belial.

"Enough," said Lucifer. "Thank you, Detective. I'm looking forward to our next conversation."

"Yeah, same…I think."

Wayne holstered the gun and left the park. Lucifer turned in the opposite direction towards the other exit and Belial started to follow.

"It's a mistake to rely on humans," said Belial.

"Maybe so, but he has information that can prove useful to us," said Lucifer. "As he just demonstrated."

"The thing about John the Baptist? Why's that important?"

"Angels—even fallen ones—are nothing if not predictable," said Lucifer. "That *Paradise Lost* quote? That fits. But this reference to the Baptist doesn't. And something that breaks pattern is something we should take into serious consideration."

"He's jumpy and suspicious," said Belial. "The angels spent centuries brainwashing humans into believing you're the root of all evil. You really think you can convince him otherwise?"

"He's a pragmatist, he'll come around," said Lucifer. "At the end of the day, we're dealing with a vicious killer and Cooper cares about people. He'll check up on me, but then I believe he'll realize I'm his best shot at stopping Astaroth."

CHAPTER 17

When Anael stepped off the elevator and walked into Eden, she felt a kind of tension in the air. There were eyes watching her, but she mostly ignored them and went to the bar where she inquired about Uriel. The bartender told her he was upstairs and waiting for her.

Anael walked up the spiral staircase to the next level. This room was equipped with a private bar, and Uriel stood behind it, filling a glass with whiskey. His blue eyes rested on her for a minute, and then he turned his attention back to his liquor.

"You summoned me?" she asked.

"I did," he said before draining the glass. He paused after throwing back the whole drink, then refilled. "I wanted to know why you haven't accomplished the mission you were given."

"I spoke with him already," she said. "I tried to explain the dangers of him remaining here on Earth, but he wouldn't listen to me."

"And when you spoke to him, did you by any chance happen to mention my name?"

"What does that have to do with anything?"

Uriel scoffed and drained the second glass. "Because he was here."

"Lu—The Adversary set foot in Eden?"

Uriel nodded while he poured himself another whiskey. "He did. And he wasn't too happy about the way I—how did he put it—'exploited' your connection to him."

"Is that what you were doing?" asked Anael.

"Don't really see how that matters, do you? The point is he came here looking for a fight. He's becoming unhinged, which is exactly what I wanted to prevent."

"You provoked him. You had to know there would be consequences. The Adversary's not one for doing as he's told. He hasn't been that way for a long time. I don't see why you thought this would go any differently."

"At the very least you could have kept my name out of it."

"And say what? That I came down from Heaven under my own cognizance? He would have seen right through a lie like that. He knows where I stand. Besides, I don't recall you ever mentioning that your involvement was some kind of secret. Perhaps if you weren't such a coward—"

Uriel's head jerked up and his eyes flared with azure power. "You hold your tongue, Anael!"

Anael didn't flinch in the slightest at Uriel's outburst. She rested her hands on her hips and stood firm, staring right back at him. No display of power was needed on her part—just her very poise spoke volumes.

"You asked me to try to get him to return to Hell. You thought our connection would make him more willing to listen to me than any other. I warned you this would happen, but you were insistent, so I did as I was ordered. He refused—just as I told you he would. And lest you've forgotten, our deal stated that if he refused me, I would return to Elysium. Yet I still remained, willing to try again. Now you're making me wonder if I was right to do so."

"You still think you can convince him, then?" asked Uriel.

"Of course not. But if it means I can go home without your incessent prodding, then I'm willing to try again."

Uriel shook his head. "You seem enthusiastic about your prospects. What hope do you have if you've resigned yourself to defeat before you've even begun?"

"Maybe none."

Uriel sighed and continued to drink. "I think there's more."

"What do you mean?"

"I felt a surge of power recently. It bore Lucifer's signature. I get the sense he's searching for something."

Anael approached the bar and took an empty glass. She poured herself a drink and held it up so Uriel could see. "Hope you don't mind, seeing as how you never offered me one."

"I'm not exactly feeling like a gracious host at the moment."

"Oh yes, I can clearly see that." Anael sipped the whiskey. "You say the Morningstar is searching for something. Do you know what it is?"

"Unfortunately, no. But knowing Lucifer, whatever it is, I'm sure it's trouble for all of us." Uriel moved away from the bar and towards the platform overlooking Eden. He slid one hand in his pants pocket as he sipped the drink. "I'm curious about your meeting with him, though. You've told me the outcome but not the details. Did he say anything, give you an indication of what he might be planning?"

Anael leaned against the bar. The memory of her discussion with Lucifer wasn't a pleasant one. The first time they'd met in centuries had just opened old wounds. Wounds that she'd thought fully healed long ago.

"The way he talked, I got the impression that the only thing he's searching for is pleasure. Embracing his desires to the fullest extent possible."

"Unchecked desire can be a dangerous thing. It was his desire to rule that led to The Fall in the first place."

"To hear him tell it, he had no interest in ruling."

"He *actually* said that?" Uriel chortled.

"Did I miss the joke?" asked Anael.

"The Adversary, who led a rebellion in order to overthrow the Divine Choir. Who sought to usurp the throne of the Presence. That same creature told you he didn't want to rule. It's so preposterous."

"You're the one who wanted to know what he told me. Don't blame the messenger, Uriel."

"It's not what Lucifer said that worries me." Uriel turned his back to the view of Eden and focused his eyes on Anael once more. "You almost sound like you believe him."

Anael's head snapped to attention and her tone sharpened. "I said no such thing."

"You didn't have to. It's *how* you said it."

Anael rolled her eyes. "Maybe you've spent too much time amongst mortals. If there was anything in my tone, it certainly wasn't intentional. You're reading too much into things."

"The last time angels bought into Lucifer's lies, it caused a war. I hope you're not foolish enough to go down that path, Anael."

"My loyalty is to Heaven, as it's always been."

"And now's your opportunity to prove it," said Uriel.

"You expect me to confront Lucifer again."

"No. At least, not at first. Instead, I want you to investigate this energy surge I felt. Try to learn just what he's up to and what he's searching for. Maybe we can get to it before him."

"Fine," said Anael. "But after this I'm through. I go back to Elysium and you never call on me again."

"I don't think that will be a problem." Uriel turned his back on Anael and sipped his drink. "You're dismissed."

He waited until he heard Anael's footsteps move down the stairs. Once they drifted into silence, he went back to the bar. The Divine Choir tasked him with seeing to it that Lucifer was dealt with, one way or the other. In truth, they believed the best course of action was to simply destroy him.

But Uriel wasn't so certain. While the Choir may have felt that the Infernal Court wouldn't side with Lucifer after his abdication, and though Uriel had made Lucifer believe he felt the same, the fact of the matter was he really didn't. Before The Fall, Lucifer was everyone's favorite angel. Beautiful, strong, confident. And most of all, charming.

That charm was what Uriel feared most about the Morningstar, even to this day. He'd managed to turn obedient soldiers into enemy combatants using nothing more than a silver tongue. Even after his abdication, Uriel couldn't risk the possibility that Lucifer still inspired his old army. Whether he wanted this job or not, Uriel's responsibility was now the guardianship of the Earth. And he would see to it that nothing threatened it.

Anael seemed the most efficient solution. The angel Lucifer had loved above all others, the only one whose counsel he had ever truly considered. But now, Uriel was starting to have doubts about her ability to complete the mission. What would happen if Lucifer somehow managed to twist even her over to his side?

If it came to that, Uriel feared the Choir might be right and the only way to deal with the Morningstar was to destroy him. It was a sobering thought, which was why Uriel left his empty glass on the bar and started drinking directly from the bottle.

CHAPTER 18

Wayne pulled his car to a stop in the driveway and shifted into park. He sat there for a few minutes and just stared at the large mansion in front of him. A place this big for just Lucifer—or Lucifer and Belial, assuming they lived together. Seemed extremely wasteful. But then again, he was technically royalty, so it made sense for him to have a castle.

What really confused Wayne was why he was here in the first place. He knew he needed help on this case. But with Tessa out of town and Alistair back on the move, he didn't know who else to turn to. Mara certainly wasn't going to give him any additional assistance. That meant this was his only choice.

After a sigh, Wayne reached to the passenger seat, where two sealed evidence bags rested. He picked them up and turned off the engine, then got out of the car and walked up the path to the front door. Wayne rang the doorbell and waited. A few moments passed and then he pressed the bell again. There was still no answer. He sighed and looked up at the mansion.

"Should've called first, Coop…" he muttered to himself.

Just when he was about to return to his car, the door opened. Belial stood in the doorway and crossed his arms, looking down at Wayne. Didn't seem like his demeanor had become any cheerier since the last time they saw each other. Belial just stared at him, saying nothing.

"You wanna let me in or would you rather we just gaze into each other's eyes all night?" asked Wayne.

Belial turned away from the door and called out into the home. "The meatsack is here to see you."

Lucifer appeared a few moments later and smiled at Wayne. He moved past Belial and offered his hand. Wayne was still hesitant being in Lucifer's presence, but he shook the hand anyway.

"Thank you for coming down here, Detective Cooper. I know it's not as convenient to get out here, but I appreciate it," said Lucifer.

"Don't mention it." Wayne held up the evidence bags. "The offer still good?"

"Yes, of course. Come right in. Would you care for something to eat? Or a drink perhaps?"

"Wouldn't say no to a beer."

"Wonderful." Lucifer looked up at Belial. "Could you grab two beers and bring them into the library?"

Belial nodded and disappeared down the hallway. Lucifer led Wayne into the library and sat down in one of the two large chairs near the fireplace. Wayne remained standing for a few minutes and studied the books on the shelves.

"Pretty impressive collection," he said.

"I've barely begun reading them," said Lucifer. "But I felt I should start, so I bought a large assortment of random titles. I've only gotten through a few so far. I plan to eventually read every single book on these shelves."

"So the Devil came to Earth to read books…" muttered Wayne.

"And to watch movies, play video games, interact with people, and so on." Lucifer waved his hand to indicate that the list was not exhaustive. "I'm retired, Detective Cooper. I plan to enjoy my retirement by living for myself. For pretty much the first time in my life."

Belial entered the lounge and handed one beer bottle to Lucifer. The other he put on a small table beside the empty chair. Wayne walked over to the table and claimed the beer. He watched as Belial left the room.

"Your bodyguard's not a fan of humans, is he?"

"Bit of an understatement, wouldn't you say?" asked Lucifer. "But no, he's not. Belial doesn't think much of my retirement plan. He doesn't understand the appeal of this place or humans in general."

"But you do?"

"I've watched your kind from afar for centuries, Wayne. I've always been envious of how you were born with free will. Whereas my kind, we have to fight for it."

Wayne sat in the empty chair across from Lucifer and sipped his beer. "I made some calls. Spoke to Alistair and Tessa."

"And…?"

"They weren't exactly leaping over the moon while singing your praises, but they also said they believed you were on the level."

"I suppose that's the best one could hope for. We are dealing with a pretty unorthodox situation."

"More than anything, I think they were more ticked off at the fact that you're up here and Cross is down there.

They didn't seem to have much against you personally outside of that."

"That's understandable. But there's a price for everything and I feel like Cross was a good choice for my successor," said Lucifer.

"Why him? As the big guy is proof of, you've got no share of demons who will do what you say."

"That's the problem, isn't it?" asked Lucifer. "They'd do what I say. That position requires someone independent, with the will to do what's necessary. Not simply a soldier following orders."

Wayne didn't offer a response, just sipped his beer and stared at the empty fireplace. The talk of Hell always made him visualize flames. Even though he knew now from those who had been there that it wasn't what Hell really was. But he still couldn't fight the perception left by a lifetime of the stories and culture. And the same was true of the man—or whatever he was—that sat across from him calmly drinking a beer.

"Jeremy Raines," said Wayne, now looking at Lucifer. "You know who that is?"

"Sounds vaguely familiar. Why?"

"Young guy found near Lust. Face was burned, babbling incoherently about the Devil's vengeance. Witnesses said they saw him attacked by a guy with wings," said Wayne. "We didn't have anything else to go on, so had to let it drop. Told Tess about it and that's when I first heard you were up here."

"Ah yes, the would-be rapist," said Lucifer. "I remember him now."

"He wasn't a demon, was he?"

"No, he was human. A poor excuse for one, but human nonetheless."

"So why?" asked Wayne.

Lucifer tilted his head to a slight degree. "What do you mean?"

"Why did you attack him?" asked Wayne. "He wasn't a demon, so he wasn't one of your escapees or whatever. Wasn't anything supernatural about him at all. So why did you care?"

Lucifer cocked a brow. "Are you saying I *shouldn't* have stopped the rapist?"

"Of course not," said Wayne and sighed. "I'm just trying to get a handle on you. Cross once told me that demons feed off human corruption. Something about the negative energy generated by their actions."

"That's true, particularly demons on the lower rung of the totem pole," said Lucifer. "But I'm not a demon."

"So you're still an angel?"

Lucifer closed his eyes and took another drink. After the sip, he stared at the label on the bottle. "When a soul is corrupted by Hell, that soul becomes a demon. It's true of humans and it's also true of angels. All of The Fallen who rebelled against Heaven with me—like Belial and Astaroth—they're all demons."

"But you're different," said Wayne. "Doesn't that mean you're still an angel?"

"I still have my wings, but my eyes show I've experienced Hell's touch. Maybe it's punishment from the Divine Choir to remind me of what I'd lost. Maybe it's because I isolated myself from the rest of Hell's people. I've entertained both theories as well as a thousand more. Sitting alone in a tower for eons gives you a lot of time to think," said Lucifer. "Whatever the reason for my current existence, I don't really know *what* I am anymore."

"So you're not quite a demon, you're not quite an angel, and you don't need to feed on negative energy," said Wayne.

"Raines was going to deprive that young woman of what I value more than anything else—free will. I fought a war because of it. I couldn't stand it, so I chose to act. Though I admit I might have been a bit harsh."

Wayne shook his head. "Maybe not. Seemed like the little prick had it coming."

"But enough about that. Let's discuss why you came," said Lucifer. "Can I see the evidence?"

Wayne set his beer on the small side table and handed the evidence bags to Lucifer. Working carefully, Lucifer opened the first bag and reached inside. It was a watch stained with blood.

"That watch belonged to Alan Gibson, the first victim. He was wearing it during the attack."

Lucifer wrapped his fingers around the watch and propped his elbow on the armrest. He closed his eyes, concentrating on the task. Wayne watched as the Devil's face contorted and twisted, wondering all the while just what the watch was showing him. He wanted to ask Lucifer what he could see, but he was also afraid of interrupting the process.

A sigh escaped Lucifer's lips and he opened his eyes before putting the watch back in the bag and then resealing it. He passed it back to Wayne and gave a shake of his head.

"Nothing, I'm sorry."

"You couldn't see *anything* useful?" asked Wayne. "Even if it's just a body type or whether the killer is male or female. The smallest detail could be more helpful than you imagine."

"I understand that. But when I say nothing, I mean I *literally* saw nothing. No flashes, no impressions, nothing."

"Is that normal?"

"Based on my limited experiences using my ability on Earth? No." Lucifer stared off at the ceiling. "Maybe time's a factor...the impression could conceivably have faded. Or handling, considering the number of people who have come into contact with it."

Wayne picked up the second evidence bag. "Care to try another?"

Lucifer nodded and accepted the bag. He opened it and reached inside. This was a small gold crucifix with a matching chain attached. Lucifer pulled it out by the chain and dangled it, studying the spinning cross.

"Can you touch that?" asked Wayne.

Lucifer gave Wayne a look of annoyance. "Don't be ridiculous."

He pulled the cross up by the chain and grasped it in his hand. Once more, his eyes closed and Wayne watched as Lucifer concentrated. Again, his head moved, creases forming in his face. But as before, Lucifer opened his eyes just a few moments later. He dropped the crucifix into the bag, sealed it again, and passed it back to Wayne.

"So nothing at all?" asked Wayne.

Lucifer took the beer and sipped. Judging from the expression on his face, Wayne gathered that he wasn't used to things not going his way. At feeling so...powerless in a situation such as this. Wayne could sympathize. More than once in his career, he'd felt like that when an investigation had hit a dead end.

"I only took one object each from the evidence room. Thought it would be less suspicious that way if anyone had noticed," said Wayne. "I could go back, get something else."

"I don't think that matters," said Lucifer. "I'm starting to wonder if this is intentional."

"You mean Astaroth's found a way to block you?"

"In a way. The spell I tried, it couldn't produce a location like it was supposed to. He may have found a way to block anyone from discovering too much about him."

"Is that it then?" asked Wayne.

"No," said Lucifer. "Astaroth is my responsibility, and I'll see to it that he's brought to justice no matter what I have to do. I promise you we'll figure something out."

"I hope you're right." Wayne stood up and reached inside his jacket. He took out a business card and set it down on the table, then placed his finger on it. "If something else turns up or if your vision thing is…I don't know, delayed or whatever…do me a favor and give me a shout."

"I will. Thanks again for stopping by." Lucifer rose and offered a handshake. "I'm only sorry I couldn't be more help."

Wayne accepted it. "Ditto. But shit happens, not much you can do about it. I'll go ahead and let myself out, you have a good night."

He took one final swig of the beer and left the bottle on the table. Wayne backtracked from the library to the foyer, seeing Belial standing near the front door with his arms crossed. If not for his eyes following Wayne, one would be forgiven for thinking he was a statue.

"Catch you around, big guy." Wayne opened the front door on his own and walked from the mansion and back to his car. He climbed into the driver's seat and shook his head. "Half-demons, warlocks, vampires, and now Satan himself is my co-pilot. I gotta get a new line of work."

CHAPTER 19

There was no easy path to follow in order to trace whatever spell Lucifer had done. Remnants of the magical energy lingered, but nothing enough that could form a clear. In hopes of trying to pick up the scent, Anael rode the 'L' train around the city. Flying would of course be easier, but she wanted to keep her profile low.

But the trail had proven fruitless. She'd spent the whole day riding each line of the CTA's train system. There were the occasional traces, and when she came across one of those, she'd get off the train, but would quickly find it had faded or wasn't strong enough to indicate a clear path.

Whatever Lucifer was after, Anael began to get the sense that it wasn't an object, but something more abstract. The train wasn't really giving her any sort of help, so she decided to get off at the next stop, which was Addison. While descending the steps from the train platform to the street below, Anael saw a crowd of people on the streets. She moved in closer to see what the reason was and saw they were coming out of a sports venue just down the street. Their enthusiasm was infectious and she couldn't help but wonder why simply watching men play a game inspired such emotionally-charged reactions.

Anael turned her attention away from the crowd of baseball fans, and something caught her eye. A newspaper rack stood on the sidewalk, with the latest edition of the *Chicago Sun-Times*. The headline on the front page was impossible to miss—"CLERGY KILLER CLAIMS THIRD VICTIM."

She grabbed the handle and pulled, breaking the lock on the machine and then reached in to take one of the papers. Anael unfurled the paper and began reading the top story. A sense of dread went through her as she absorbed the details of the killer's actions.

Uriel told her not to confront Lucifer yet, but Anael felt something wasn't right and she wouldn't get answers any other way. Still holding the paper, Anael went into an alley and her wings emerged from her back as bright, azure energy. Before even fully forming them, she wrapped herself in their luminous glow and vanished from the Wrigleyville area.

Anael reappeared standing on a beach. Her wings opened and then retreated into her back. She heard a yipping sound coming nearby. Anael looked to it and saw a tiny dog—little more than an overgrown rat, she thought to herself—snarling and barking at her. The dog was on a leash held by an old woman who just stared unblinkingly at the angel.

Anael ignored both and started walking from the beach towards the road. She was in the Lakeshore Historic District now, and the home Lucifer had bought for himself was nearby. Their last conversation hadn't gone too well, so Anael thought this time she'd show Lucifer the courtesy of at least knocking first.

The house wasn't hard to find, and she walked up the

path to the front door. Anael pushed the button for the bell and waited as she heard it echo from beyond the door. When it opened, she was surprised to see not Lucifer, but a tall man with a bald head and glowing yellow eyes. Even in the human form he'd constructed for himself, Anael could still recognize the soul inside as one of The Fallen. He evidently recognized her as well, because he snarled once he looked at her.

"Belial..." she muttered. "What are you—"

The demon didn't even wait for her to finish her sentence. He grabbed Anael by the throat and pulled her inside the large foyer. Belial raised her up into the air and then brought her crashing down on the marble floor, leaving a series of cracks in the tiles.

Anael struggled against his grip as he pinned her while remaining at arm's length, but he was strong enough to resist her attempts to free herself. She wrapped her legs around his neck and pulled him forward, driving his head through the wall.

That allowed her to free herself. She stood to her feet and moved into a ready pose while Belial pulled his head from the wall. He shook it, dust and plaster coming off in a cloud.

Anael lunged forward and drove her foot into his chest. The impact threw Belial back and he hit the hole his head had made. Except now his whole body broke through the wall and into the sitting room on the other side. Anael came through the hole. Just when Belial was getting to his feet, she kicked him in the head, then followed up with sweep, bringing him right back down to the ground.

Belial fell right near a coffee table. He grabbed the legs and stood, taking the table with him in a smooth motion and slamming it against her. The wood cracked from the blow and Anael was overcome with a feeling of disorientation. She tried to shake it off, but she had a case of double-vision and saw two Belials coming for her.

Anael threw punches to keep him back, but she couldn't get a proper lock on him, so her blows hit nothing other than air. Rough hands were on her body again, and the next thing she knew, she was flying through the air, thrown by Belial.

Her trip came to a sudden end when she hit something soft and firm. It was the couch, and once she hit it, it tipped back and she rolled onto the wooden floor. Anael was on her back and she heard Belial moving closer. He grabbed the couch and pushed it to the side.

Anael flipped back onto her hands and sprung forward, her feet striking him in the face. The blow caused his head to rock to the side, but otherwise did no real damage. Anael was on her feet again now and she readied for the next attack. Belial grinned at her, his yellow eyes burning with intensity.

"Fuck this," she muttered and held out her hand.

Azure flame formed in her palm and extended into the shape of a flaming sword. She pointed the tip at Belial, but he didn't seem the least bit intimidated by her weapon. His eyes burned brighter and then yellow flames formed in his own hands, creating a hellfire sword of his own that he put up against hers.

"You want to put that sword away," said Anael.

"You first," said Belial. "If you think I'm going to tolerate any angel threatening my lord, then you're in for a *very* rude surprise."

"I didn't come here for a fight," said Anael. "But if I

have to kill you in order to have a word with the Adversary, then that's something I can live with."

"You'll try, Anael. And you'll fail. Traitors aren't welcome in this house."

Anael narrowed her eyes. "The gall of labeling *me* a traitor when *you* are the ones who caused a civil war."

"That's quite enough."

The third voice belonged to Lucifer, and caused both Anael and Belial to look in his direction. They kept their weapons up, though, neither willing to concede before the other. Lucifer sighed and walked up to them. He placed a hand on each of their arms and slowly lowered them. Belial gave his master a questioning glance, but allowed him to continue.

As soon as Anael's arm was lowered, she brought it right back up. But now, she pointed the sword at Lucifer. Belial recoiled in anger and drew his weapon up and back, ready to bring it down upon her head. Just as he started to make the movement, Lucifer held up his hand.

"Belial, please. I don't like repeating myself."

"But she—"

"If you insist on referring to me as your ruler, then you should follow my commands. Wouldn't you agree?" asked Lucifer.

A low growl rumbled in Belial's throat. He retracted his sword, yet kept an angry gaze on Anael. She met his gaze with one of her own, though hers was a bit more on the smug side. No doubt that only angered Belial more. Lucifer seemed to have more respect for Anael's strength than he did for Belial's loyalty.

"Anael, if you're willing to put the sword away, then we can go in the other room and talk," said Lucifer. "That *is* why you came here, isn't it? Because if you'd rather fight, then I'm sure Belial would be happy to oblige."

"You know I'd kill him if I went all out," said Anael.

"I know you *believe* that. But I'd rather not put it to the test," said Lucifer. "Now, what's your decision—talk or fight?"

Anael glanced in Belial's direction, then met Lucifer's gaze. The soulfire blade retreated into her arm and the azure flames faded. She relaxed her body as she lowered her arm.

"Fine. We can talk."

"Very good," said Lucifer. "Belial, clean up this mess."

"But—"

"Anael came as a visitor and you immediately attacked her without saying a word," said Lucifer. "So as far as I'm concerned, this mess is your fault."

Belial lowered his head. To Anael, he almost looked like a child who had been scolded. He then turned away and went to work on cleaning up, beginning by setting the couch back in place.

Lucifer led Anael from the sitting room and back through the foyer. Anael had dropped the newspaper by the front door when Belial attacked her, and she retrieved it as they passed. He brought her into the library, where they'd spoken previously. Lucifer went to the liquor cabinet to fix himself a drink.

"So," he said as he dropped several ice cubes into a glass. He poured gin and a splash of dry vermouth over the ice, then stirred it with a metal stick. "Are you here to again try and convince me that I should return to Hell?"

"Uriel told me about your visit to Eden," said Anael.

"I thought he might. What exactly did he say?"

"That you're unhinged," said Anael. "He's under the

impression that you're plotting something. Said you were involved in some spell that made your presence felt across the city."

"And he sent you to find out what." He made an identical drink and picked up both glasses.

"Actually, he wanted me to investigate the disturbance while avoiding you. He seems to think you're after something of power."

Lucifer chuckled as he approached Anael and handed her one of the martinis. "Of course he does. Uriel wouldn't be Uriel if he wasn't nervous about something."

"Is he right?"

"Cheers." Lucifer clinked his glass against Anael's and took a sip while moving to sit in one of two high-backed chairs that faced each other in the center of the room.

"You didn't answer my question."

"Of course he's wrong," said Lucifer, then gestured to the empty chair. "Despite your statements to the contrary the last time you were here, you know I don't lie, Anael."

"I wish I could believe that. I really do." Anael sat across from him. She rested the newspaper on her lap.

"What've you got there?"

Anael held it up so he could see the headline. It seemed to make him curious and he rose from the seat to take the paper from her. Lucifer opened it up and quickly scanned through the article. While he read, Anael studied his features, trying to discern his thoughts.

"You know about this, don't you?" she asked. "It's not a surprise to you, is it?"

"Unfortunately no. In fact, I've started to look into it myself."

"Why?"

Lucifer closed the paper and handed it back to her. He slowly paced around the library while occasionally taking sips of his drink. Anael watched his movements with a mixture of curiosity and uncertainty. There was something going on with the Morningstar. Whatever his involvement with this case, Anael could easily tell from his body language that he didn't want to talk about it. Perhaps because he feared how she would react?

"Lucifer…" she said as she stood.

He looked at her with wide eyes full of both surprise and hope. It had been reflex. Anael didn't even realize it until she saw his expression. She had given voice to the name she swore to never speak again.

To his credit, Lucifer said nothing. His expression was all the attention he drew to the issue. Anael felt embarrassed enough as it were, so she was grateful that he chose to simply move on.

"I'll tell you what's going on," said Lucifer. "But I need you to listen with an open mind. And though I hope it would go without saying, what I'm about to say is not to leave these walls. Do we have an understanding?"

Anael sighed. "If you're going to reveal anything about some plot that could endanger the balance—"

"No, nothing like that. In fact, it's precisely the opposite," said Lucifer. "Though it may not seem like that at first, just listen until the end."

"Okay," she said. "Tell me everything."

CHAPTER 20

Despite asking her to keep an open mind, Lucifer had expected Anael's reaction to his story to be one of anger. What he *hadn't* counted on was the punch she threw at him. Or the strength behind it. Powerful enough that he was surprised his head was still attached to his neck.

Lucifer fell back on the floor and rubbed the spot on his jaw where Anael's fist had connected. The glass had fallen out of his hand and landed on the carpet. It didn't break, but it did spill his drink. He looked at her while moving his jaw around to make sure it was still in place.

"I suppose I had that coming."

"You're damn right you did." Anael's hands were still clenched into fists. Her wings had flared out as well and her eyes burned with power. Her voice was raised as she spoke. "How many souls escaped Cocytus?"

"If you're asking for an exact number, I'm afraid I can't help you there. But more than one and that's enough," said Lucifer.

"And one of them is here killing clergy members." She gritted her teeth. "All so you could selfishly abandon your station."

"My Lord!" The doors to the library were thrown open and Belial stood on the other side. He saw Lucifer on the ground, and then his gaze found Anael. He growled and took a menacing step inside. "I feel you've caused enough damage today!"

"Stop!" ordered Lucifer before rising to his feet. He picked up the glass and went to the bar to refill his drink. "It's okay, Belial. I actually had it coming."

"You heard him," said Anael. "Go back to cleaning up the mess you caused."

"I'll use your skull as an ashtray, you winged bitch," muttered Belial.

"Stop posturing, Belial. You don't even smoke," said Lucifer. "Please, leave us alone to talk."

Belial gave one last look at Anael and said, "This isn't over between us. Not by a long shot."

"You're welcome to try any time your master lets you off the leash," said Anael.

Belial turned his back, muttering something under his breath. He slammed the doors shut behind him. Anael placed her hands on her hips and retracted her wings, then glanced in Lucifer's direction.

"What did he say?" she asked.

"No doubt pointing out the irony in your last comment," said Lucifer. "After all, aren't you on just as much a leash as him? Only yours is held by Uriel."

"I told you that I came to you despite Uriel's command."

"Yes, you did. But something tells me he would have wanted you to come after me eventually. You're still here acting in service of his larger orders to send me back."

"How can you still insist on even staying here after what you just told me?" asked Anael. "You left Hell and without your presence, Cocytus was weakened. Now some of Hell's criminals are out and about. And your pride still won't allow you to admit to your mistakes?"

"I didn't *know*, dammit!" he snapped back. "Had I known, I would have—"

"What?" Anael scoffed. "Don't tell me, you would have stayed? Given up your chance for freedom?"

Lucifer turned his back to her and took a sip from his glass. It was a nice sentiment, but was it really one he believed? He'd wanted nothing more than to escape Hell and have an existence that was all his own. When the opportunity arrived, he didn't even give it another thought. Just gave his throne away and left for Earth.

"I would have…prepared," he said. "Found some way to fortify the prison. I never wanted any of this, Anael."

"Just like you didn't want the rebellion. Or Hell's throne," said Anael. "Don't you see? These things came about because you were too arrogant to think about the potential consequences of your actions. But everything has a cost. You've seen that firsthand. You've borne those costs yourself. And yet, even still, you think the rules don't apply to you."

"No, I think the rules shouldn't exist in the first place."

"That's not for us to say."

"Maybe not. But that's how it should be."

"If wishes were horses, beggars would ride."

"What do you want of me, Anael?" asked Lucifer. "I made a mistake. I'm trying to fix it."

"And how exactly do you plan to do that?"

"I'll track down every demon that escaped Cocytus and destroy them, one by one."

"You have another responsibility. First you have to fix

the damage caused to the prison. You need to strengthen those walls so no one else can escape," said Anael.

Lucifer sighed and refilled his glass. "If only it were that simple…"

"It is," said Anael. "You go back to Hell. You take up the throne again. If you think the cambion will put up a fight, then I'll see to it you have some assistance."

"What, you'll talk with Uriel? Put in a good word for me with the Divine Choir?" asked Lucifer. "Yes, I could easily take the throne back with your help. But the Choir wouldn't do something like that out of the goodness of their hearts. On the contrary, they'd take that opportunity to make Hell a puppet state. I'd be right back under their thumb again and everything I've spent eons fighting for would be gone. May as well summon the Angel of Death to kill me where I stand."

"You made mistakes. Maybe it's time you faced some consequences."

"I'm already facing them," said Lucifer. "Even if I took back the throne—against every instinct I have—it wouldn't be enough. The power I used to create Cocytus was my own. That power is gone."

Anael's hardened expression softened and she lowered her hands to her sides. "What are you saying?"

"I don't have the power of an archangel anymore," said Lucifer. "If you wanted to, you could probably kill me yourself. You could take me prisoner without much trouble if that's what you wanted."

"You can't be serious."

Lucifer returned to his chair and settled into the seat. He crossed his legs and slowly sipped his drink. "I really wish I were lying, Anael. But it's unfortunately the truth.

I can't fix Cocytus, all I can do is track down the demons who have escaped."

"But if your powers are weakened, how are you going to stop them?"

"Erebus is watching over the prison, far more closely now. And Belial has vowed to remain on Earth until all the escaped demons are dealt with. What remains of Cocytus should be capable of holding the rest in. Only the most powerful ones likely managed to escape, and they were few and far between."

"Do you know who this one is?" asked Anael, picking up the newspaper.

"I believe I do. The energy Uriel detected, that was a spell used to learn the demon's identity. I'm fairly certain what we're dealing with is Astaroth."

"He was one of The Fallen, wasn't he?" asked Anael. "The one who tempted the Nazarene?"

"The same," said Lucifer. "He brought us the closest to war we'd been since Lilith. I couldn't abide that, so I banished him to Cocytus. Now he's escaped."

"And you're sure he's the one behind this?"

"More or less."

"Not exactly instilling me with confidence," said Anael.

"The 'less' part is because there's something strange about his behavior," said Lucifer. "The first victim, there was a reference to *Paradise Lost*, about reigning in Hell versus serving in Heaven. But the second was a reference to Salome asking for the head of John the Baptist, presumably just because the victim's name was John. It feels like a forced attempt at a religious reference and that's not Astaroth's style."

"What's the reason for it then?" asked Anael.

"I wish I knew. Let me see that again."

Anael passed him the newspaper and Lucifer read through each line of the article. When he finished, he handed it back to her.

"The paper didn't print any explicit details, probably because the police are still keeping them under wraps."

"Why would they?" asked Anael.

"They tend to keep things out of the paper, withhold details or even give false ones. It's a way of deterring false confessions. If someone confesses to the murders but only uses the details found in the paper, you can bet they're innocent. But if they mention the details no one but the police knew, then they know they've got their man."

Anael rubbed the back of her neck as the distance between her eyebrows shrank. "You mean there are people who confess to crimes they never committed? Why would anyone do such a thing?"

"What can I say, humans are a pretty strange breed," said Lucifer. "I've spoken with the detective in charge of the investigation. He's agreed to contact me with any further details he finds. So I imagine we'll be hearing from him shortly about this latest victim."

"There's something else you haven't considered," said Anael. "As I recall, Astaroth is no slouch in the power department. Are you sure you and Belial are enough to take him on by yourselves?"

"Shouldn't be a problem. I think Astaroth may be possessing a mortal. As you said, he's powerful, so he should be able to create a form on his own. But if he hasn't, that can mean one of two things. Either he felt it would be amusing to possess a human—"

"Or he's still weakened from the escape and physically

can't create a body for himself," said Anael.

"Exactly, and I think the latter is more likely than the former."

"How do you know?"

"Something Belial said. He didn't understand why a demon like Astaroth would *want* to inhabit a human when he didn't have to, and there was a kind of sense it made. Astaroth doesn't care as much for the corruption of humans as he does for getting revenge on Heaven."

"What if you're wrong and he *is* possessing a human because he wants to?" asked Anael.

"Then admittedly it'll be more of a challenge, but not impossible," said Lucifer. "Together, Belial and I should be more than capable of dealing with Astaroth."

"And then?"

Lucifer gave her a quizzical look. "And then what?"

"You stop Astaroth, what will you do with him? You must know you can't take him back to Cocytus, not if it's too weak to hold him. Maybe not immediately, but in time he'd find the strength to escape once again, and then you're right back where you started."

"There's only one thing I *can* do. I have to kill him," said Lucifer.

She raised an eyebrow. "*Kill* him? You're serious? You'd kill one of The Fallen?"

"Wouldn't be the first time," said Lucifer.

"I know, but this isn't Abraxas," said Anael. "Back then, you had the backing of the Infernal Court. How would they react to you going after one of The Fallen now? Especially after you turned your back on them?"

"As far as I'm concerned, they don't need to know. Neither does the Divine Choir." Lucifer looked up from his drink. "I think you understand my position, don't you?"

"Why would I?"

"Because Astaroth's escape—all these escapes—would be viewed poorly by the Choir. And they may want to take matters into their own hands. Which could inflame tensions between Heaven and Hell. That would be bad for all of us, and you know that just as well as I."

"You're right," said Anael. "But if you're going to try to kill one of The Fallen in your current state, then Belial might not be enough. That's why I'm going to help you."

Lucifer blinked several times at Anael. "Excuse me? *You* are going to help *me*?"

"You're right about the potential for things to get out of hand. I don't have any desire to see another celestial war in my lifetime. And if Astaroth is indeed powerful, then you and Belial might not be enough," said Anael. "Plus I want to see to it that this is done right."

"You think I'd trust you watching our backs?"

"I do, because you already trusted me with all this information, knowing I could take it right back to Uriel," said Anael. "So are you willing to put aside our differences and work together?"

Lucifer kept his smile hidden. "Yes, I think I am."

CHAPTER 21

Wayne Cooper stood outside the entrance to the Cook County Medical Examiner. Lucifer had called him, asking about the third victim, and Wayne told him to meet here after-hours. He didn't want too many eyes focused on this case, particularly if one of those sets of eyes belonged to Janice Wagner. Even after he'd asked her to wait and think if she really wanted to know the truth, she was still pressing him.

Truth was, Wayne hadn't decided if he would tell her even if she was seriously invested in the truth. He'd always thought he'd wished someone would have given him the choice. But as a detective, Wayne couldn't help trying to discover the truth behind things. Even if he had the choice, he would have chosen knowledge over ignorance. Janice seemed much the same, and nothing he could say would deter her.

Out of the corner of his eye, Wayne caught a flash of light. He went around the side of the building and saw Lucifer approaching him. By his side was a beautiful young woman. Her long, dark hair and fair skin matched that of the Morningstar, but in her eyes was where the difference truly lied—her bright, azure eyes stood in sharp contrast to Lucifer's burning yellow ones.

"Figured if you brought company, it'd be the big guy," said Wayne, giving the woman a sideways glance. "The less people involved in this arrangement, the more comfortable I'd feel."

"I understand your concern, Wayne. Do you mind if I call you Wayne?"

Wayne shook his head. "I really couldn't give less of a shit. What I care about is why you're bringing someone else into this."

"Anael is an old friend. And she has just as much interest in seeing Astaroth eliminated as the two of us."

"So what is she?" asked Wayne, looking her over. "Another demon like that Jason Statham lookalike you were with last time?"

Anael grabbed Wayne by the collar of his leather jacket. He held up his hands while his eyes betrayed shock and anger.

"Take it easy, lady!" he said. "The jacket's got sentimental value."

Lucifer sighed. "Let him go, Anael. Wayne is our ally here."

"He called me a demon," said Anael.

"An honest mistake. You *are* hanging out with the Devil, after all. What do you expect?" asked Lucifer.

Anael's nostrils flared and she released her grip. Wayne took a step back and straightened his jacket. He was starting to think retirement was looking pretty good. Had fought it for a while, but it was increasingly becoming more tempting with each passing day.

"I'm sorry I called you a demon," said Wayne. "If it's any

consolation, it's not a commentary on your appearance."

"Flattery is wasted on me, mortal," said Anael.

Wayne glanced at Lucifer. "So if she's not a demon then what is she?"

"She's an angel," said Lucifer.

Wayne blinked several times, then gave a chuckle. "An angel and a demon walk into a morgue. Already feels like the setup for a bad joke." He sighed and shook his head. "So why are you teaming up with an angel?"

"As I said, Anael has just as much interest in stopping Astaroth as the both of us," said Lucifer.

"Fine, let's go inside."

Wayne walked to the front entrance with the two following and opened the doors. Most of the lights in the forensic center were off at this time of night, but Wayne had made a deal with the ME to come in after-hours with a consultant. He was an old friend, so he agreed. They stopped at the elevators and Wayne pushed the call button.

"So this Astaroth guy, Lucifer said he tried to tempt someone important to the angels." Wayne glanced at Anael. "Who's so important that a demon trying to tempt them would call in the big guns?"

Anael looked at Lucifer. "He doesn't know, does he?"

"I felt meeting the Devil was shock enough for one day, so I chose to withhold some things," said Lucifer.

The elevator arrived and they all stepped inside. Wayne hit the button and then asked, "Feel like I'm not in on the joke here."

"The man that Astaroth tried to tempt wasn't a man at all," said Anael. "He was a nephilim."

"Nephilim? Wait, you mean like…"

"Yes, just like Dakota Reed's child," said Lucifer.

"He knows about that?" asked Anael.

Lucifer cocked his head in Wayne's direction. "A friend of the cambion. It's sort of how we became acquainted."

"So there were others?" asked Wayne.

"In the early days, there were many. When both Heaven and Hell realized their power, we exterminated them," said Anael.

The doors opened and they walked down the hall.

"But then at one point, Heaven became worried that humanity wasn't converting to their side fast enough. So they decided to send an angel to try converting people. His bright idea was that a child of angel and man could do the job better than any celestial, particularly if he were raised properly," said Lucifer. "In Hell, this was seen as a violation of the armistice."

"The angel acted on his own," said Anael.

"Or so they say," said Lucifer.

Anael glared at him. "It's *true*."

"Regardless, the Infernal Court was hung on what action we should take. They were pissed, seeing it as a double-standard."

"Despite all the demon offspring who walk the Earth…" muttered Anael.

"You know just as well as I do that Heaven is much more structured than Hell," said Lucifer. "And besides, there's no real comparing a nephilim to a cambion."

Wayne halted his stride and held up his hands. "Could you stop with the sniping? Just tell the damn story."

Lucifer glanced in Anael's direction. "Perhaps if I'm not interrupted…"

Anael huffed and hung back a few paces while Lucifer

and Wayne started walking on ahead and Lucifer continued the story.

"I chose neutrality. By that point, I'd stopped caring about Heaven or what they wanted to do with humanity. I just wanted to keep my domain intact and my people safe, even if that meant leaving Earth to Heaven's influence."

"Let me guess, Astaroth had a different idea," said Wayne.

Lucifer nodded. "He wanted to corrupt the child, bring him over to our cause. He'd tried several times when the boy was in his teens and early twenties, and even came close a few times. But the boy resisted, growing into a man. And by that point, Astaroth was growing frustrated. He made one last attempt at corrupting the nephilim, but he resisted. And so, Astaroth saw no other choice. While in disguise, he drove a spear into the man's body."

"A spear?" asked Wayne. "Thought nephilim were made of tougher stuff than that."

"This was no ordinary spear. It was enchanted, a weapon capable of killing even a celestial being," said Lucifer. "So the man died. Heaven wanted blood, but the nephilim's death actually helped them far more than they could have hoped for. They settled for Astaroth being imprisoned within Hell's prison."

"Some of this is sounding kind of familiar…" muttered Wayne as they came up to the door for the examination room. "Who was this nephilim anyway?"

"We called him the Nazarene," said Lucifer. "But I believe you have another name for him."

Lucifer opened the door while Wayne stood there slack-jawed. "Holy shit. You don't mean…?"

"Let's have a look at what we've got here," said Lucifer

as he approached the gurney with the body lying on it. He pulled the sheet back and looked down into the face of a man whose skin had sagged with weight and age.

Wayne moved past the gurney over to a counter where a file rested on the surface. He picked it up and started flipping through the contents, glancing up to see that Anael had now caught up to them. She closed the door and leaned against it, folding her arms and staring at the body.

"Same MO as the others. Tortured with an edged weapon before being killed," said Wayne. "The papers are calling him the Clergy Killer now, but I'm guessing since you reached out, you already saw the headline."

"I can see why you chose detective as your profession," said Lucifer.

Wayne scoffed. "Hilarious. Anyway, guy's Stanley Barrett, another priest. This one at Holy Family in Little Italy."

Lucifer looked up from the body. "Little Italy… So am I correct in assuming this is another Catholic church?"

"Now who's the detective?"

Lucifer scoffed himself and looked back down at the body. "Knife attacks again?"

"Yeah."

"What's significant about the Catholic church?" asked Anael.

"All three were Catholic priests, each one found in a different church," said Wayne.

"And each one accompanied with a reference to a passage of some kind," said Lucifer. "Did you find one here?"

"Yeah." Wayne went back to the counter and took a plastic bag. Inside was a piece of paper. "In fact, this time he decided to be a bit more direct."

Lucifer took the the bag and examined the paper. "'*Las-*

ciate ogne speranza, voi ch'intrate.'"

"You know what that means?" asked Wayne.

"It's Italian," said Anael. "Or rather, very old Italian."

"She's right. And the translation is, 'Abandon all hope, ye who enter here.' It's the inscription on the gates of Hell in Dante's *Inferno*."

"So we've got two quotes that have to do with Hell," said Wayne. "Those two both fit. But that one about John the Baptist doesn't."

"What was that one?" asked Anael.

"The second victim was named John, his head was cut off and that reference was left behind," said Wayne. "But what it means, we still don't really know. It doesn't really fit in with the others."

"In the Bible, the Baptist was killed because Herod offered Salome whatever she wanted," said Anael.

"Yes, that she did…" Lucifer moved away and started to think about how these connected with Astaroth. "I think I'm beginning to understand it now."

"How so?" asked Wayne.

"Astaroth was a firm believer in the rebellion. Even after The Fall, he remained fully committed to his beliefs. It's why he saw Heaven's creation of the Nazarene as an act of utter hypocrisy and why he chose to strike out."

"He believed in *you*. Not the rebellion, but the angel who started it," said Anael. "That's what you're missing."

Lucifer raised his head, his eyes widening. "I was wrong."

"Been waiting a long time to hear you say those words," said Anael.

"The second victim," said Lucifer, ignoring the angel's comment. "I thought it was out of place. The reference to the Baptist's beheading seemed so strange when compared to the Milton quote. But now I actually see how all three fit together."

"How's that?" asked Wayne. "The first and third are about Hell, but the second has nothing to do with it."

"The *Paradise Lost* quote was about the pride of choosing to rule Hell over serving Heaven. And then the Bible quote references a king who granted a terrifying request without consideration. Now the *Inferno* quote means the loss of hope," said Lucifer. "They're all about me."

"You think Astaroth is trying to send you a message," said Wayne.

"Either that or he's simply lashing out," said Lucifer.

"Except he's not choosing just anyone," said Anael. "He's specifically targeting Catholic priests."

Lucifer tried to consider that. She was right, the priests didn't quite fit in with the other references. Why not just any victims if Astaroth was working through his anger towards the Morningstar? Why specifically did he want to go after these priests?

"All three were found around the same area, weren't they?" asked Lucifer.

"Close by at least. Not too far off."

"Points to possession," said Lucifer. "If Astaroth had created a body for himself, he wouldn't feel any attachment to one particular area."

"Still leaves the question of why this profile for the victims," said Wayne.

"Perhaps the host has something against Catholic priests?" asked Anael.

Now Wayne was the one whose eyes had widened. "Goddammit, she's right." He reached into his jacket and took out his cell phone, then quickly dialed. Once he heard the voice on the other end, he started speaking quickly. "Wagner, it's Coop. Yeah, I know, we can talk later. Meanwhile, there's something I want you to look into. I think I've found a damn good lead. Search for people in the city who have made allegations about abuse at the hands of clergy. Concentrate on the areas where the victims were found. I'll explain later. Call me if you find anything."

He hung up and found Lucifer and Anael staring at him with anticipation. "What is it?" asked Lucifer.

"Do you pay much attention to the news down in Hell? A vendetta against Catholic priests isn't so surprising given the revelations over the past several years," said Wayne.

CHAPTER 22

"Not much else we can do other than wait," said Wayne, but then he motioned to the body. "Unless, of course, you feel like trying your little laying-on-hands trick again."

"What's he mean by that?" asked Anael.

Lucifer just shook his head. "I doubt it'd be much use. Astaroth seems to have found a way to block my sight."

"What sight?" asked Anael.

"Psychometry," said Lucifer. "Though it doesn't appear to work on Astaroth's victims for some reason. I think it's because he's found a spell to keep himself hidden form me."

"You should still try though," said Anael. "If there's any potential way to find him, we have to try it."

Lucifer moved closer to the body. He knew she was right. But more than anything else, it was his injured pride. Whenever he tried to use his ability and saw nothing, he felt impotent. Once he was among the most powerful beings in the universe. Even as an angel, Astaroth was on the lower rungs, not among Lucifer's lieutenants. And after being imprisoned for centuries, he would have been weakened. Yet still, he was powerful enough to block Lucifer's sight.

He didn't say anything as he raised his hands and gently

set them on Barrett's body. Lucifer tried to concentrate on Astaroth's memory, an attempt to see if he could kick-start the ability that way. But as much as he tried to reach out, to find his former soldier, he just couldn't.

There was no connection. And perhaps that was Lucifer's fault when he made the decision to isolate himself. Now he was absolutely powerless to do anything about Astaroth's reign of terror.

He moved away from the body and kicked a rolling tray of medical instruments in anger, then slammed his fist against the morgue drawers. Wayne stepped forward and held out his hand to try and calm Lucifer.

"Ease up, okay? The ME's not gonna be anxious to do me more favors like this if you go around kicking shit."

"It doesn't work," said Lucifer. "The sight…I can't see anything."

"It's fine, we'll find another way," said Wayne. "Like I said, my partner's—"

"Oh please." Lucifer gave a chuckle of condescension. "Astaroth is in the driver's seat of whatever body he's possessing. He's not going to give a damn what the regular occupant has been through. Entertaining this is just a way to make you feel like you have something to offer."

Wayne huffed, his face reddening as his lips tightened. Lucifer could sense what he was feeling and it was to be expected after a comment like that. Lucifer moved closer to him, narrowing his eyes.

"Is that anger, Wayne? How does it feel to know just how useless you really are? Maybe you should have just retired, gone on to do something else with your wasted life."

"Should probably remind you that *you* came to *me* for help," said Wayne.

"Because I thought you might have some degree of competence," said Lucifer. "But it seems I was wrong about that."

"I'm not the one whose Satanforce or whatever conveniently stopped working."

Anael stepped between the two men, holding her hands up. "This is getting a bit too tense."

"Coming from you, that's hilarious," said Lucifer.

Anael shot Lucifer a hard glare and then said, "Detective, I'd like a few minutes alone with the Adversary. If you don't mind."

"You two nearly got into it once already. Think I'm going to leave you alone to tear this place apart with some angel slapfight?"

"What would it matter?" asked Lucifer. "You couldn't stop us even if a fight *did* break out."

"I've about had my fill of you right now…" muttered Wayne.

"Detective, please," said Anael again, a pleading tone in her voice. "Just a few minutes. I promise we won't fight."

Wayne looked hesitant, but he decided to comply with Anael's request. "I could use a cup of coffee anyway."

Before speaking, Anael waited until Wayne was gone and reasonably confident he was out of earshot. During that time, Lucifer could feel the tension between them. In some ways, it seemed even worse than when she appeared by the side of his pool.

"You're an asshole," she said.

"My secret's out then," he quipped in response.

"You're not angry with him or with me. You're angry at yourself."

One of the things Lucifer both loved and hated most

about Anael was her insight. She could always tell what he was feeling, even if he denied it to himself. And it appeared that their time apart hadn't dulled that skill in the least.

"You're blaming yourself for all this. For Astaroth getting free, for being unable to find him, and that means you're putting those deaths on your conscience."

"I'm not interested in psychoanalysis, especially not from someone who can't be trusted," said Lucifer.

"Still on that?" asked Anael.

"I'll be 'on that' until the stars burn out," said Lucifer. "I've been willing to entertain you, but the fact of the matter is you betrayed me."

"You were planning to destroy the very foundation of what divine society was built on. I couldn't stand by and do nothing as you tried to corrupt others with your insanity."

"So you wanted people to go on living the lie, that the Divine Choir truly had an audience with the Presence even though none had ever confirmed its existence? They always spoke on its behalf, but it never issued orders directly. None had ever seen it. And you think we should have still worshipped that without question."

"You have no proof of this, Morningstar."

"I had Metatron's words. No one knew more about what the Divine Choir was up to behind closed doors than the Scribe."

Anael shook her head. "I was hoping that perhaps you'd come to some semblance of sanity after this. Your willingness to help Cooper, to find Astaroth, it seemed that for once, you'd begun taking responsibility for your recklessness." Her gaze steeled as she locked her sight on Lucifer. "Now I see I was being naive. You're pathologically incapable of accepting responsibility, Morningstar."

"What would you have me do, Anael?" asked Lucifer, throwing his hands up. "I tried. You saw me place my hands on the body. You saw me try and use my powers. I. *Can't.* Find. Him. So what would you like me to do now?"

"For once in your life, I want you to put aside your pride and just *listen.*"

Lucifer moved away from the gurney. He leaned his back against the door and folded his arms across his chest. "Very well. The floor is yours, Anael. I'm all ears."

"What I was going to say is I came with to help you and that's exactly what I plan on doing," said Anael. "Your power may be diminished, but mine isn't. If you're willing to accept my help, then I can channel my power through you, use it to boost your own abilities."

"And you'd do that?"

"There's a catch," said Anael.

"Isn't there always?"

"Our souls would touch. And I don't mean that in some poetic sense, I mean it literally. What that means is we'd become linked. Just like how part of your essence has touched all the prisoners of Cocytus, except this would be stronger."

"In other words, you would have a method of tracking me," said Lucifer. "Perhaps even monitoring me."

"And you'd have the same," said Anael. "If we wanted to, we could make life very difficult for each other. Which is why we'd need to trust each other if we were going to do this."

"That's the problem right there, isn't it?" asked Lucifer. "How can I ever trust you again?"

"I was thinking the same thing." Anael sighed. "I know what this must sound like."

"Yes, I'm sure you do. It sounds like you're trying to trick me into giving Uriel an all-access pass to my life," said Lucifer. "I won't be put on a leash, Anael. And I'm not fond of righteous blowhards watching my every move."

"Notice how I haven't run off to tell Uriel about what's happening here?" asked Anael. "We both want Astaroth gone, Lucifer. We both want this balance restored. But if we're going to do that, then you have to accept some consequences for your actions. Just as, I suppose, I do as well."

"You're asking far too much of me. And I can't do it," said Lucifer.

Anael slowly exhaled. She was trying to control her own anger bubbling up inside. But Lucifer knew this was the way it had to be. Her offer of help now seemed more transparent than ever. It was all just a ploy in order to gain his trust. Then, when the time was right, she would have betrayed him again. But he wasn't going to allow that to happen again.

"Perhaps it's best if I handle this on my own," said Lucifer. "I'm certain Cooper's idea will be able to yield some useful results. So thank you, Anael, but I think I'll pass on your suggestion."

"You're a prideful idiot, Morningstar," said Anael. "This isn't the way to end things. And I promise you that you *will* regret this."

Azure light emerged from her back, forming into the shape of wings. They wrapped around Anael's body and transported her away in a bright flash. Lucifer walked over to the spot where she stood and reached his hand out. Had she still been there, he would be touching her right this moment. But he had forced her away, just like before.

The door opened and Wayne had returned holding a

cup of coffee from the vending machine. He scanned the room with a perplexed look on his face. "So where'd the angel go?"

"I have no idea, nor do I care," said Lucifer.

"In that case, I think we're done here," said Wayne. "I've pretty much had my fill of Heaven and Hell for tonight."

"And just what do you think you're going to do about Astaroth?" asked Lucifer. "You aren't capable of taking on a demon, let alone one as powerful as him."

"Maybe not. But I'm also not going to be demeaned by the likes of you," said Wayne.

"'The likes of…'" Lucifer repeated the phrase in disbelief. "I came to you with an offer to help you find Astaroth."

"You came to me because you were out of options and you needed help," said Wayne. "I'll call up Tessa again, she if she'll be back in town soon or if she can put me in touch with someone else who can help. But I don't think I'll be turning to you again at any point in the near future."

"You're making a profoundly stupid mistake, my friend."

"He's your responsibility," said Wayne. "If you want to stop preening and start owning up to your bullshit, then more power to you. Until then, you're no longer part of this investigation. Do we understand each other, Mr. Prince of Darkness?"

"Yes, I believe we do. Good luck, Cooper. You're going to need all the world can offer if you have a hope of surviving Astaroth."

Lucifer walked past Wayne and out into the corridor. He left the building and stepped outside into the crisp night air. Yellow light emerged from his back, taking shape and forming into feathered wings. But instead of simply teleporting himself back home, Lucifer's wings raised him off the ground. He flew above the city, bathing in the moonlight and relishing the feel of the cool air as it blew across his face.

He felt free. High above it all, away from the humans, the angels, and the demons. Maybe that's what he lost sight of when he made the decision to come up here. Isolation from the rest of the universe, that was where true freedom lied. He'd been fooling himself into believing that he could find happiness in anything else.

That was the key. Let Cooper and Anael deal with Astaroth. The Morningstar was finished.

CHAPTER 23

After dealing with Lucifer and Anael, Wayne wanted to put all this insanity behind him, go home, and get some rest. He'd hoped sleep would bring some new clarity to the situation, but it didn't seem to work out that way. Instead, he just woke up still as annoyed as when his head hit the pillow. There were still no leads in the case, so he took a personal day. After he called the station, he turned off his phone and didn't dare open his computer. He stayed inside the whole time and did nothing but watch TV.

The day after, it was time to get back to work. He'd hoped a day of unplugging from everything would have improved his mood, but it was just a slight reprieve. Now he felt just as frustrated as before.

Wayne went through his morning routine of showering and preparing breakfast. As he stood over his kitchen sink, chewing on a piece of toast and washing it down with hot coffee, his cell phone started to ring. Wayne set the coffee down and swallowed the mouthful of bread, then answered the phone.

"Cooper."

"It's Wagner," came Janice's voice on the other end.

"Are you coming in today?"

"Yeah, about to head out actually," said Wayne. "Do you have something?"

"It's about that thing you asked me to check up on. I'll show you what I've found when you get here."

"All right."

"And Coop? That *other* thing we talked about…?"

Wayne rolled his eyes. "Okay, fine. I'll tell you whatever you want to know."

"Good. I'll see you when you get here."

Janice hung up and Wayne set his phone on the counter. He finished the toast and then quickly drank the rest of the coffee. After pulling on his leather jacket and holstering his gun, Wayne took his phone and left the apartment.

As he drove from his apartment to the station, he kept thinking about what Janice had said. For years, Wayne had been known as the freak chaser, the one who was always interested in the strange cases nobody else wanted to touch. But after dealing with Cross and now Lucifer, Wayne was pretty sure he'd had enough. He'd been fighting letting Janice in on what he knew. But she was determined and if she wanted to be the new freak chaser in the CPD, he was ready to pass the torch.

Once inside the station, Wayne didn't even have a chance to reach his desk before Janice came up to him. She spoke quickly about how she'd scoured records all day yesterday. By the time they reached his desk, Janice was setting down a print-out of a newspaper article on his desk.

"There were a few different allegations in the area," she said. "A lot of them accused this guy, Father William Dixon. He worked out of Holy Family, but get this? He also did some guest-speaking at Pompeii and Procopious."

"What happened to him?" asked Wayne.

"His victims brought a class-action lawsuit against him and the Diocese settled out of court. This was about ten years ago." Janice opened her folder and produced another print-out, this one a court summary of the case.

"And then?"

"One of the victims wasn't very happy with the settlement because of the confidentiality agreement that was included." Another piece of paper, this one another article. "Sean Grady later said that he'd been coerced into signing it by the lawyers and the other victims. He sued to invalidate the gag order, but the Diocese's lawyers kept throwing up procedural motions to extend the case. Grady eventually dropped the suit because he couldn't afford to keep it going."

"The American legal system for you. If you've got the money, you can tie things up in litigation and bleed your enemies dry…" muttered Wayne. "What happened with Dixon?"

"He retired shortly after the settlement was reached. And then a few years ago, he was found dead in his home." One more article, this one an obituary for Dixon. "Cause of death was ruled a suicide."

"How'd the timeline fit with Grady?"

"Grady was in court when Dixon killed himself. His friends and relatives said he'd been distraught ever since Grady brought the new suit forward. Some say he was feeling extreme guilt and that's what drove him to it."

"Or he was afraid Grady would get the gag order lifted and then all his dirty laundry would be aired out in full view of the public," said Wayne.

"Whatever the case, Grady went pretty quiet after that.

I was able to find an address for him, though."

The last piece of paper Janice produced was a print-out of an Illinois driver's license sporting Grady's name and an address in Fuller Park, just a few miles away from where the murders had taken place.

"This is great, Wagner. Thanks."

"And the other thing?" asked Janice.

Wayne set the piece of paper down. This was the time to tell her everything. He got up and led her away from his desk and into an empty interrogation room. Wayne closed the door behind them and leaned against it, then gestured for her to sit. Janice chose to simply lean against the table and folded her arms.

"What I'm about to tell you is not exactly a secret, but it's also not something that's usually spoken about," he said. "This city is...unique. And I'm not talking the kind of unique that can be chalked up to city pride. There are... things here that you might not be aware of in other places."

"Like whatever attacked Jeremy Raines," said Janice.

"Exactly."

Wayne went on to lay it all out for her. How he came to be associated with Luther Cross, what that association had led to, and all the other assorted craziness that had occupied his life over the past few years. To her credit, Janice seemed to take it all in stride. As he went through the story, he couldn't tell if she was shocked, bored, or even listening. Her face was completely unreadable.

"So what about Raines?" she asked. "You think a demon did that?"

"No, I know what did that—or rather, who."

"And? Why aren't you going after them?"

"Because no judge would grant an arrest warrant based

on a bunch of people seeing a guy with wings and burning eyes," said Wayne. "More than that, this guy is someone you probably *don't* want to get mixed up with."

Janice gave a snicker. "You sound like you believe Raines' story that he was attacked by the Devil himself."

Wayne didn't laugh. And once Janice realized why, her smile dropped and her jaw hung loose.

"You're kidding."

And then Wayne brought her up to speed on Lucifer and who was really behind these murders. That time, she didn't take it in stride as much. Hearing that the supernatural was real and there were helpful demons and monsters, that was one thing. But hearing that Satan had moved into an Evanston mansion and was getting into arguments with angels? That had elevated this to an all-new level of crazy.

"Jesus Christ…" she muttered.

"Yeah, about him…" Wayne was about to offer up more revelations. But when he saw Janice's face, he decided against continuing with that story and just shook his head. "Y'know what, it's not important."

"How do we stop a demon?" asked Janice. "Especially now that you've pissed off the Devil? I can't imagine that leading to anything good."

Wayne shrugged. "Maybe, maybe not. I've got someone I can call, see if they can help us find someone else who does this kind of thing. But first, we need confirmation that we actually *are* dealing with a demon here."

"And how are you going to get that?" asked Janice.

"Grady seems like the most-likely suspect. So, I'll go have a chat with him," said Wayne. "Luther taught me a few tricks to kind of suss out if a person's being possessed. I'll get the confirmation, then see about finding an exorcist."

"Are you sure that's smart?"

Wayne scoffed. "Hell no. But what choice have I got? Even if we got an arrest warrant on Grady, wouldn't do a whole lot of good. The demon could break out of any handcuffs easily. And if he decided that Grady was just too much trouble, he could simply jump to the nearest warm body."

"You can't go alone," said Janice.

"I'll be fine," said Wayne. "Look, I'm going to go have a word with Grady, and then I'll give you a call."

"And if you don't?"

Wayne sighed. He didn't want to think about that, but she had a point. If he brought her along to back him up and the situation went south, she'd be in it as much as him. But an insurance policy couldn't hurt.

"I'll check in at the bottom of every hour," he said. "If you don't hear from me, there's a false bottom in my desk drawer. In it, you'll find a notebook. It's where I keep some numbers in times like this. You call the number for Tessa Kang, let her know what happened and she can help you out, okay?"

Janice nodded. Wayne opened the door and started to leave the interrogation room. But before he stepped back into the hall, Janice called out to him one more time.

"Be careful, Coop."

"Don't worry, not the first time I've faced off against a demon," said Wayne. "Everything'll be fine, trust me."

Wayne sat in his car across the street from the Fuller Park house that was listed as Sean Grady's address. On the passenger seat was a book Luther had given him once about demonic possession. Wayne picked it up and flipped through to the earmarked sections. He'd read the book from cover to cover on several occasions, but he'd never done this on his own and he wanted to be sure he had things right. Of course, he didn't intend to perform the exorcism himself—he still had to find someone able to do that. But he wanted to be certain.

He took a bite of his bagel as he continued watching the front door. There was no one home when he arrived and so he grabbed a coffee and a bagel for lunch and waited. The morning had passed without incident or appearance and eventually got well into mid-afternoon.

Finally, he saw a car pull up in front of the house and park on the street. Wayne checked the print-out of the driver's license. It was definitely Grady, no question about it. On the floor of the passenger seat was a small box. Wayne picked it up and opened it, retrieving a bottle of holy water and a crucifix. There was no way of knowing if it would be much help against a demon like Astaroth, but Wayne kept telling himself that he just needed some sign that Grady was possessed. Even a flicker of the eyes would be enough to tell him this was the guy.

Wayne climbed out of the car and crossed the street to Grady's house. He quickly ran up the stairs and rang the doorbell. There was no answer at first, so he pushed the button a second time. Still nothing, so Wayne started knocking on the door. Finally, it opened, and Wayne focused on Grady's eyes. Grady, for his part, just stared back with a mixture of curiosity and annoyance.

"Something you need?" he asked. "*You* knocked on *my* door, y'know."

"You Sean Grady?" asked Wayne.

"Why?" asked Grady, straightening and leaning back. "What do you want?"

Wayne showed him his badge. "Detective Cooper, Chicago Police. I'd like to have a few words with you, if you don't mind."

Grady hesitated for a minute and Wayne put his badge into his jeans pocket. He left his hand down at his side, right near his holstered weapon. If Grady rabbited or tried something else, Wayne wanted to be ready.

But then, Grady broke into a light chuckle and held the door open wider. "Well in that case, come on in."

Wayne was suspicious of the sudden change in attitude and he wasn't sure if it was the best thing to go inside. But he kept telling himself that all he had to do was play this off as a simple cop doing a routine check. He didn't have to say anything that would let Astaroth know he was onto the truth. And the best way to do that was to just be civil for the time being. So he walked into the house and Grady led him to the living room. There was an old loveseat and a beat-up recliner with patches of black masking tape. Grady gestured to the loveseat while he plopped down in the recliner.

"Sorry about that," said Grady. "Thing is, I've been ducking some debt collectors."

"They harassing you?"

Grady shook his head. "Nah. Not yet, at least. So far it's just been letters and phone calls. But I'm expecting visits to start up soon enough." Grady shook his head and chuckled. "Sorry, where are my manners? You want anything? Glass of water or I can put on a pot of coffee…?"

"No thanks."

"I've got some beer in the fridge if you like."

Wayne held up his hand. "Can't, not while I'm on duty."

"Oh right, right," said Grady. "So what can I help you with, Detective?"

"Have you heard about the Clergy Killer?" asked Wayne.

"The…what?"

Wayne raised an eyebrow. "I'm guessing you don't pay much attention to the news."

Grady shook his head. "Not really, no. Why?"

"Well, as the name suggests, someone's targeting members of the clergy, a serial killer. There have been three victims so far, each one in a different Catholic church around Pilsen. The latest was in Holy Family. I did some digging and I found out that you were involved in a class-action lawsuit against them. About abuse suffered at the hands of William Dixon."

"Yeah, that's right," said Grady. "So what, you think I killed those guys? Because I wasn't able to get justice from Dixon?"

"Actually, just doing a routine check." Wayne could detect the tension rising in Grady's tone, so he was very deliberate with the words he chose.

Grady scoffed. "Y'know, that sonnuva bitch got off light. If I'd had what I do now…"

"And what do you have now, Mr. Grady?"

Grady smiled. "Oh, I've got a new friend, Detective. You see, he doesn't get out much. I keep him on a pretty short leash. But I think with you, I'll let him come out to play."

"'Short leash?'" asked Wayne. "What the hell are you talking about...?"

Grady chuckled in response. "You wanna see for yourself?"

CHAPTER 24

Lucifer stood in front of the liquor cabinet dressed in a burgundy robe. He took the bottle of bourbon from the shelf and examined it, then looked at the empty tumbler in his other hand. With a scoff, he tossed the glass to the side and it fell on the floor, shattering. Bottle in hand, Lucifer went back to his chair and fell into it. He pulled the cork out and began drinking straight from the bottle.

His phone had rang a few times, but he grew tired of its noise and now it lay in pieces in the corner of the library. On the small table beside him rested a copy of *Beyond Good and Evil* and he picked it up again, turning to the earmarked page. But after a few minutes of reading the words, Lucifer tossed the book over his shoulder.

He had no interest in reading philosophy or anything else. Nor did he find the idea of watching a movie or playing a game to be entertaining. Not even the thought of going out and indulging in physical pleasures appealed to him. There was a restlessness brewing inside him. Astaroth was still out there, but Lucifer had decided that Anael and Wayne could deal with him on their own. They'd find him, Anael would then have to report the situation to Uriel, and there'd be contention between the Court and the Choir.

But Lucifer now knew it didn't matter. Neither side *really* wanted war, so they'd find some way to save face. They always did. It wasn't his problem, not anymore.

The doorbell started to ring. Lucifer tried to ignore it as he drank the bourbon. Finally, after a few rings, he shouted out, "Belial! Door!" The ringing continued unabated. Lucifer took another swig from the bottle and again shouted, "*Belial!*"

"My apologies," came the demon's reply.

Lucifer heard Belial's footsteps between the sounds of the bell. Finally it was silenced, replaced by muffled voices that he had no real desire to make out.

"It's someone for you, Morningstar."

"Unless it's a pizza, I'm not interested," said Lucifer.

"Sorry, no pizza. But I *do* need to talk to you."

This was a new voice, and Lucifer's curiosity was piqued. He stood from the chair and looked at the new arrival. A woman dressed in a dark suit with chin-length brown hair. She also held up a badge that identified her as a detective with the Chicago Police.

"If this is about a donation to the policeman's charity, I'm afraid I'm tapped out for the…century," said Lucifer. "You can try me again after that."

"My name's Janice Wagner, I'm Wayne Cooper's partner," she said. "Or…kind of."

"Then I'm *certain* I'm not interested in whatever you have to say," said Lucifer. "Unless, of course, you were lying about the pizza."

"Coop's been missing since this morning," said Janice.

"Did you try the donut shop? If I've learned anything from TV, it's that cops love donuts," said Lucifer. "That and shooting unarmed minorities without cause. Oh…do you think maybe he's doing that?"

Janice huffed. "You're trying to get a rise out of me, aren't you?"

Lucifer chuckled and leaned against the chair, drinking straight from the bottle again.

"Coop told me everything," she said. "I know who you really are, Lucifer."

"Did he also tell you that I told him to fuck off?"

"Yeah, I got that part. But then he went missing. He was looking into a possible suspect and he told me that if he didn't check in, I should call the names in this book." Janice reached into her jacket and took out a pocket-sized notebook. "Unfortunately, I didn't get any hits. There weren't a lot of names in there, and the ones that were either couldn't get here or didn't answer the phone. But there was a business card in here as well—yours."

"And?"

"And I know this may be a long shot, but I need your help to find my partner," said Janice.

"If Cooper is in danger, that's his own fault. I want nothing more to do with any of this shit," said Lucifer.

"As I understood it, the reason this demon is running around killing people is because you decided to take early retirement," said Janice. "So I'd say my partner being in danger is definitely *your* fault. At least in part."

"What do you want from me, Wagner?" asked Lucifer. "I couldn't help."

"Maybe not before, but you could help now. Stop this demon before it kills again. Before it kills my partner," said Janice.

"Think I'll pass," said Lucifer. "I didn't come here to

play hero, I came to enjoy my life for once."

Janice gave Lucifer a once-over and then shook her head. "All I see is a pathetic sack of shit drinking alone in a bathrobe while bitching about how bad his life is. Which, I should add, he's doing from the comfort of a damn mansion. It might be funny if it weren't so sad."

Lucifer scoffed and took another swig, then sat back down in his chair. "Belial, show the detective out. And from now on, let's make a new rule—no one is allowed through that door unless they have a pizza."

"Fine, I'll go." Janice took the card from the notebook and left it on the liquor cabinet. "But in case you change your mind, the guy's name is Sean Grady. Think Coop was right about the church abuse angle, and he went to confront the guy. I left the address on the back of your card."

Lucifer scoffed. "Go ahead and leave your trash here. I'm sure Belial will take care of it."

Janice left the library and Lucifer continued chugging the bottle. Not long after he heard the door close, he finished off the last of the bourbon and threw the bottle over the back of the chair. He sighed and leaned back into the cushions.

"You know, I don't care much for these humans," said Belial, sitting down across Lucifer. "But they do on occasion have something of note to say."

"And what exactly would that be, my friend?"

"You said you came here to enjoy yourself, but doesn't seem like you're doing much of that right now," said Belial.

"What do you want from me, Belial?" asked Lucifer. "I'm no hero. Hell, I'm not even a proper villain. I'm a failed revolutionary who spent eons moaning alone in a tower over my loss."

"And exactly how is your current state any different?"

Lucifer narrowed his eyes, then stood up and went over to the bar. "Whose side are you on anyway?"

"Yours, my Lord. Always."

Lucifer turned and pointed at Belial. "I thought I told you not to call me that."

"You did, repeatedly." Belial crossed his legs and looked at the empty fireplace. His yellow eyes burned and flames appeared within the enclosure. "You remember when we were still in Heaven?"

"I try not to." Lucifer looked over the bottles in the cabinet. "Do I feel like vodka or rum…?"

"I was an archai," said Belial. "I was nothing."

It was true, the archai were the lowest order of angels. Essentially they were administrators, serving the whims of their superiors. Lucifer of course remembered it well, but he didn't care much about what Belial had to say. He took a bottle of vodka and examined the label, frowned, and put it back.

"Maybe a nice rosé…" he muttered as he found a bottle of wine. "No, needs to be chilled first."

"I would have lived out all of eternity remaining in that station, never even having the opportunity to rise above," said Belial. "And that's when I met you. The first time I saw you, I was in awe. You were the Morningstar, the most beautiful of all the angels."

"Yes, I do cut quite a dashing figure." Lucifer took a bottle of Jose Cuervo. "Tequila…hmm…"

"I never believed I'd be worthy enough to stand in your presence, let alone speak to you," said Belial. "And yet, you told me I wasn't limited to this station. That despite the decrees of the Divine Choir, I could be something more. I could be what I wanted."

"Yeah, I was an idiot back then." Lucifer took the cap off the tequila bottle and started to drink straight from it. He cringed a little after he stopped and shook his head. "That burns in all the right places…"

"You were right, Lucifer. You were the Morningstar, the only angel in all of creation who had the courage to stand before the armies of Heaven and proudly and defiantly tell them to fuck off."

"'You *were* the Morningstar.'" Lucifer repeated as he sat in the corner of the chair. His back was half on the seat and he draped a leg over the armrest. "Why are you speaking in the past tense?"

"Because I don't see the Morningstar sitting across from me. I see the coward who's taken his place."

Lucifer's nostrils flared and he sat upright. "Care to speak up, boy? I don't think I heard you quite so well."

Belial stood up and grabbed the bottle from Lucifer. The Morningstar protested and reached for it, but Belial shoved him back into the chair, then threw the bottle into the fireplace. The flames flared up upon contact with the tequila. Lucifer looked into those flames, almost as if he were mesmerized by them.

"Fire, that's what you once represented," said Belial. "Powerful, consuming. But you've allowed the Choir to contain you. Your refusal to accept responsibility allowed them to paint you as a villain for eons. You threw out the rulebook once before. Now you have the opportunity to do it again, to write your own legend. The Morningstar I believed in, the one I proudly followed into the depths of Hell, the one I dedicated my existence to serve—he wouldn't reject that opportunity. But what will you do?"

Lucifer stood and walked back over to the bar. He picked up the card Janice had left and examined the Fuller Park address written on the card. "Maybe you were right. Maybe the Morningstar is gone and in his place is just the Adversary. Nothing but the subject of stories created to keep the masses in line."

"You rebelled because you wanted freedom. But if you allow them to continue to write your story, then you may as well still be a servant in Heaven," said Belial. "Astaroth is your responsibility, Lucifer. Regardless of your reasons for imprisoning him, his escape is on your head. And the deaths he's caused are also your responsibility. You have to be willing to take the next step, to bring him down before you can ever truly find your freedom."

Lucifer's eyes began to glow. A bright light shone around his body and the robe began to change. It moved over his skin, twisting and mutating until it settled on the form of white slacks, a black button-down shirt, and a white jacket. He turned around and looked at his charge.

"You're right," said Lucifer. "Perhaps it's time I took back my own destiny. Redefine who I am and what I stand for. And I can start by cleaning up this mess."

"I'll be right by your side the whole time," said Belial.

"No, that's quite all right," said Lucifer. "I want you to return to Hell for the time being."

"But my Lord…"

"Astaroth is just one of many who escaped. There are others, and I need you to learn whatever you can about them," said Lucifer. "I'll take care of Astaroth and you'll find out where we'll go next."

Belial nodded. "Yes, of course. But are you sure you

have the strength to face off against Astaroth on your own?"

"Maybe, maybe not. But I have to do this on my own."

Lucifer's eyes began to glow again and wings emerged from his back. They wrapped around his body and in a flash of light, he was gone.

CHAPTER 25

On a house-lined street in Fuller Park, a bright, orange light appeared and quickly expanded. It took the form of Lucifer, with his wings wrapped around his body. As the wings opened, they maintained the bright glow and receded into his back. Once they were gone, the night returned to normal.

Lucifer walked up to the front door and rang the bell. There was no answer. He tried again, but was left with the same result. Not even slamming his fist several times on the door drew any attention. Finally, he sighed and kicked.

The door splintered under the force of his foot and what remained of the wooden construct swung inward on its hinges. Lucifer stepped inside and looked around the house, his eyes burning brightly in the darkness.

"Astaroth, I know you're here," said Lucifer. "I think we've both had enough of these games, don't you?"

No answer came. Lucifer knelt down and placed his hand on the hardwood floor. He stared forward, the intensity of his eyes burning brighter as he concentrated. It was strange—in this close proximity, he should have no trouble sensing Astaroth. He could feel him, he knew he was near, and yet it still felt like he was distant at the same time.

Almost as if Lucifer were trying to look at him through a dense fog.

But it wasn't enough to hide him anymore. Lucifer could still make out the shape, even if he couldn't see the features. And he knew where Astaroth was. Lucifer rose to his feet and walked down the narrow hallway beside the staircase. There was a door beneath it and he reached for the handle, opening to reveal stairs leading into a dark basement.

Lucifer descended the steps, the glow of his eyes illuminating the path. When he reached the foot of the stairs, he could hear a muffled voice. Lucifer turned his attention to the sound and saw Wayne sitting on the ground. Both his hands and feet were cuffed around a water pipe that was connected to both the floor and ceiling, and he had duct tape over his mouth. Lucifer went over to him and pulled the tape off. Wayne cringed and worked his jaw to mitigate some of the pain.

"Didn't expect to see you here," he said.

"Thank your partner." Lucifer broke the chain on the cuffs around Wayne's wrist, then did the ones on the feet. "Where's Astaroth?"

"He was here a minute ago," said Wayne.

"What did he do to you?"

"Nothing." The way Wayne said that made it seem like he didn't really believe it himself.

"Nothing?" Lucifer repeated the word, this time as a question. "Why wouldn't he kill you?"

"Because you don't kill the bait."

Lucifer stood and turned. He saw a young man standing there, holding a large butcher knife in one hand, and Lucifer could see Wayne's gun sticking out of the front of his pants. As he looked at the man, Lucifer narrowed his eyes, trying to see inside. He still couldn't figure out why when the host was standing right in front of him, Astaroth's presence was still obscured.

"So, this is Sean Grady. Or his skin, at least," said Lucifer. "Couldn't create a body of your own, Astaroth?"

Grady smiled. "I knew you'd come. He told me you would."

"'He'?" Lucifer raised an eyebrow and then glanced over at Wayne, who was now standing himself.

"Been talking like that ever since I got here," said Wayne. "As if he's working with someone."

"I…think I'm beginning to understand," said Lucifer. "You really *are* Grady. And Astaroth…"

Grady smiled. "He's in here. He's been a lot of fun to play with. Given me plenty of tools so I can get back at the ones who made me. Who allowed it to happen."

"What the hell's going on here?" asked Wayne.

"This isn't a case of a demon possessing a human. It's a case of a human *trapping* a demon," said Lucifer.

Grady smiled and started to unbutton his shirt with his free hand. When he opened it, Lucifer could see scars carved in the shape of a sigil. The kind of sigil meant to contain a demon. Astaroth was trapped inside this man.

"That's why I couldn't get a clear sense of Astaroth. He wasn't blocking me, he was hidden," said Lucifer. "Locked away inside this human form."

"Very good, Morningstar," said Grady. "And through him, I learned so much. I experienced the memory of how good it felt to have the Nazarene's blood drip onto my hands as I drove the spear into his side. I decided I should continue where Astaroth left off."

"But if it was you the whole time, then why those messages?" asked Lucifer. "Why were you trying to goad me?"

Grady chuckled. "Would've thought that'd be obvious by now. Because I wanted to meet you. Give Astaroth a chance to kill you himself. As a thank you for everything he's given me."

"Very well," said Lucifer. "Of course, there is one problem with this scenario."

"Oh?"

Lucifer's eyes burned brightly as he extended his arms and clapped his hands together. He drew them apart and a trail of hellfire followed, forging into a sword for him to use. Lucifer held up the sword and shifted his body, moving into a battle stance.

"I don't die so easy," said Lucifer.

Grady drew Wayne's gun and squeezed the trigger three times. Lucifer deflected two rounds, but then the third hit him in the chest. It was a momentary distraction, which was what Grady needed to fire several more times into Lucifer's chest until the gun was empty.

The hellfire blade fizzled, eventually extinguishing itself while Lucifer examined the wounds that were in the process of staining his white jacket. Wayne was by his side, trying to keep him from falling over. When Lucifer looked up at Wayne, even his eyes were dimming.

"Aren't you supposed to be invincible or something?" asked Wayne.

"Suppose I'm not as strong as I'd thought," said Lucifer.

Wayne tried to keep him steady and Lucifer looked up to see Grady approaching them, holding up the knife. On closer examination, Lucifer realized it wasn't a butcher knife. But rather, it was a kind of ceremonial dagger. And judging from the symbols in it, he imagined it wasn't something that was good for him.

"Astaroth idolized you, but it seems the man doesn't quite match up to the myth," said Grady.

Wayne stepped in front of Lucifer and delivered a left hook to Grady's jaw. He groaned and shook his hand after the punch connected, clearly in pain. Grady looked at Wayne and then grabbed him by the throat. With ease, he tossed him across the basement.

"You can wait your turn, officer."

He picked up Lucifer by the throat and raised him off the ground. Grady held the blade in his hand and traced it along Lucifer's throat. Grady's eyes burned bright yellow and Lucifer could smell the stench of sulfur on him.

"I wonder, what will happen once the Devil dies?" asked Grady. "Will the heavens shake? Will the seas boil? Or will nobody even notice?"

"As a matter of fact…" said Lucifer, a spark appearing in his eyes. "I don't intend to find out."

He grabbed Grady's head and the spark in his eyes grew into a full-on inferno. Grady screamed as the entire landscape changed. Lucifer hit the ground, which was barren rock. He looked around and saw red skies. Just ahead was the edge of a cliff and a winged figure stood there looking down into the chasm.

Lucifer moved forward and the man turned. He had long, dark hair with horns protruding from his head. His skin was pale and his eyes bright yellow. The wings on his back were dark and leathery. And he was dressed in the celestial armor of an angel.

"Hello, Astaroth," said Lucifer. "I was hoping we'd have a chance to talk."

"The Morningstar." His voice carried a strange tone. Lucifer could detect the obvious disdain, but it was also tinged with reverence. It seemed that even after all this time, Astaroth still held the Devil in high regard. "I wasn't expecting to see you here."

"Neither was I," said Lucifer. "What happened?"

"The walls of Cocytus cracked," said Astaroth. "With help from others, I could break through. We all could. And we clawed our way to this world. They didn't care about you, but I sensed your presence here on Earth and I sought you out. But I was weak, not enough strength to create a form for myself. And so, I found Grady."

"And then?"

Astaroth lowered his head. "I tried to take control. But he had this strength of will, tempered through years of hardship and hatred. He was too powerful for me. So instead of trapping him within his form, he trapped me. And he could see everything I'd ever done, take my power for his own."

"He saw how to keep you trapped inside his body. Carved the sigil into his skin, locking you in."

"It's not the first time someone made me a prisoner," said Astaroth. "You cast me out. I may not have been one of the Court, but I was loyal to you, wasn't I? I fought for your cause, right?"

"You were. You did," said Lucifer. "But I gave up. I saw what my cause had done to us, and I ran away from the responsibility. I thought you could all experience the same free will as I did, and instead I just created a counterpoint for the Divine Choir. I fell prey to politics in order to maintain the status quo. And for that, I'm sorry. I never should have imprisoned you within Cocytus."

Astaroth's eyes widened. "So you'll join me? With our combined strength, we could overpower him. And then we'd be strong enough to build a new army here on Earth. Stand against the Choir once more, just as we once did."

Lucifer sighed. "No."

Astaroth tilted his head to the side. "Why not? Don't you want to end their tyranny? Free all the souls in the universe?"

"You and Sean Grady have become consumed by the past, unable to press forward. It's what gave him the strength to overpower you and what caused you to go after the Nazarene. Which only succeeded in drawing more followers to Heaven," said Lucifer. "I'm done living in the past. I won't be consumed by my failures any longer, nor will I try to ignore them. Instead, I plan on pressing forward."

"What are you saying?" asked Astaroth.

"That I'm sorry." Lucifer held out his hand and a hellfire sword forged in his palm. He raised the blade and swung it, slicing through Astaroth's neck. "But I can't allow this to continue."

As Astaroth's headless body fell to its knees, reality began to crack and fall apart. Lucifer was back in the basement and looking down at Grady, who seemed dazed by what had just happened.

"Wh-what was that?" asked Grady.

Lucifer broke free of Grady's grip. He placed his hand on the sigil carved into the man's chest. The Morningstar's eyes burned and a glow appeared in his hand. That light passed into Grady's body, concentrating around his chest. Grady screamed as the scars forming the sigil started glowing to the point that they were red-hot. They smoked and the skin popped and sizzled.

Grady screamed and fell on his back. Lucifer looked down at the man's body. There was a giant, circular burn on his chest where the sigil had been. Both it and his now-empty eye sockets smoked and the scent of burnt flesh hung in the air. Lucifer nearly dropped to the ground in exhaustion as Wayne approached him. The detective looked down at the body and then at Lucifer. The Morningstar just looked back up at him, somewhat weakly.

"What the hell happened?"

Lucifer sighed. "I killed them both."

EPILOGUE

Wayne held open the door to his apartment so Janice could enter. He closed it behind her and led her into the kitchen. For her part, Janice didn't seem to know exactly why she was here, and she kept looking around as if trying to find the answer somewhere in the surroundings.

"Thanks for coming by," said Wayne. "Go ahead and have a seat at the counter, coffee's just about ready."

There was a small kitchen island with a pair of stools on one side. Janice sat on one as she watched Wayne on the other side of the island, taking the coffee pot and pouring two cups.

"Sorry I don't have any cream or sugar," he said as he set one of the steaming mugs in front of her. "Just have to take it black, if you don't mind."

"It's fine." Janice slowly sipped the coffee and cringed a little at the bitterness. She decided to just leave it on the counter. "So why *did* you want me to come down here, Coop? Thought you still had a few more days of leave."

He nodded. "Yeah, I do. But before I announce it at the station, I wanted you to be the first to know that I've decided to retire."

"Really?" asked Janice. "But why? Did the thing with Grady shake you up?"

"In a way. Think I've known for a while that I'd had my fill of this life. But I suppose what I was really waiting for was someone I thought capable of picking up the slack once I'm gone."

Wayne opened a drawer on the island and took something out. He set it in front of Janice. She looked down at it, somewhat puzzled. It was a journal, albeit a bit worn. Janice picked it up and started flipping through the pages.

"After I first learned about what's really out there, I started keeping this journal. Every weird case, every unexplained event, it's all in there. I guess I thought that it would help me make sense of it. Keep me from doubting my sanity if I wrote it all down. But I guess now I realize that I wasn't really trying to keep myself sane, I was making a record for someone else to take over for me."

Janice looked up from the notebook into Wayne's face. His blue eyes had that same seriousness that she'd always known, but there was also a kind of resignation.

"You're serious about this?" she asked.

"You wanted to know what's really out there, and I told you some of it. And when the time came, you did the right thing by going to Lucifer," said Wayne. "So I think yeah, you're someone who can handle these weird cases. I've already left messages with some of my contacts in that world to vouch for you if you need their help, and you probably will."

Janice looked back down at the journal. Years worth of strange and unexplained investigations, all detailed in this. If anyone else saw it, they probably would have locked

Wayne away in a mental institution. But he was trusting her with this knowledge.

"Thank you," was all she could say.

Wayne smiled and sipped his coffee.

"What will you do, though?" she asked.

He shrugged as he calmly strolled from the kitchen and over to the window. Wayne leaned against it and looked out over the city. He sipped his coffee again and continued to stare as the sunlight illuminated the streets.

"I honestly haven't thought that far ahead," he said. "Just realized I should take some time for myself and enjoy what I've got."

Lucifer stood on the beach, running his bare feet through the sand and enjoying the feel of it on his skin. He closed his eyes and breathed in the scent of the lake, enjoying the cool night breeze as it blew lightly through his dark hair.

There was a new presence he sensed and he opened his yellow eyes to see her standing on the surface of the water, staring at him. Her blue eyes were glowing, and she didn't seem too happy to see him.

"Hello, Anael," he said. "I'm glad you answered my summons."

Anael gently stepped forward on the water, her own feet bare as well while the wind rippled over her white dress.

"I hope the reason you summoned me is to tell me that Astaroth is no longer a threat and that now you'll return to Hell," she said.

"You're half-right," said Lucifer. "Astaroth has been

dealt with, so there's no more danger of him. But I won't be returning to Hell."

She shook her head. "So you still haven't learned anything."

"On the contrary," said Lucifer. "I've learned that I have responsibilities to attend to. Astaroth wasn't the only escapee from Cocytus. Belial and I are already making preparations to leave Chicago for our next destination. I promise you that I'll find the others and I'll destroy them, just like I did to Astaroth."

"And then?" she asked.

He breathed deep. "And then we'll just have to see where fate takes me."

"Does that mean Hell?"

"Maybe, but maybe not," said Lucifer. "Heaven, Hell. Angels, demons. It's all so binary, isn't it? I think we'd all be better off if we just embraced the complexities of life, don't you?"

"Simplistic doesn't mean wrong, Adversary," said Anael. "Sometimes, simple is the right path."

"I suppose we'll see," said Lucifer. "And what about you? What will you do now?"

"Uriel tasked me with keeping an eye on you, so I'm going to continue to do just that," said Anael. "You can't be allowed to roam free without supervision."

Lucifer gave a sly grin. "Then I suppose I'll be seeing you around."

AFTERWORD

When I was a kid, I feared the Devil. I remember the stories from Sunday school about Hell and the Devil and one of my half-remembered memories from childhood was being frightened when I caught a bit of *The Devil and Max Devlin* on TV. Yeah, it was a comedy film (made by Disney, no less), but I was probably about five or six at the time, and seeing a red-skinned Bill Cosby with goat legs and a pitchfork surrounded by flames was enough to scare the shit out of me.

As I grew, I became more and more detached from religion. I became agnostic in high school, Taoist in college, and shortly after I graduated and moved to Japan, I just accepted that I was an atheist. And of course, my journey to atheism removed what fear I ever had of the Devil.

So why, then, was I still so fascinated by him? What was it about movies like *The Exorcist*, *Rosemary's Baby*, and *The Omen* that I found so appealing? Why did I seek out books like *Paradise Lost* and *To Reign in Hell*, or plays like *The Creation of the World and Other Business*? Why did I gravitate towards comics like *Hellstorm: Prince of Lies*, *Hellblazer*, and *Lucifer*? Why did TV shows like *Supernatural* and *Lucifer* grip me so much?

The first depiction of Heaven and Hell in other media that really grabbed my interest was Gregory Widen's 1995 film *The Prophecy*. And what really interested me was how it played with the mythology. The idea was that after Lucifer was cast out, a second war in Heaven started. This war was led by the angel Gabriel, played with near-psychotic glee by the great Christopher Walken. The movie also featured a memorable performance by Viggo Mortensen as Lucifer. And though the overall plot of the movie doesn't quite reach the heights of the premise, the Walken and Mortensen performances alone are reason enough to seek it out.

Since then, I've noticed a kind of trend throughout all the depictions of the Devil, and they all tend to revolve around the same idea—the Devil is basically a guy with a whole heap of daddy issues. Of course it's understandable why that idea is so powerful. It's extremely relatable and it gives the character some more depth and complexity as opposed to "I'm evil because it's fun, mwahaha!"

However, as I was designing the cosmology of my own supernatural world, I realized that I wanted to do something different. Something that really triggered this was "Heaven and Hell," an episode in season four of *Supernatural*. In that episode, the fallen angel Anna asks Dean Winchester if he knows how many angels have actually seen God. He believes it's all of them and she responds, "Four. And I'm not one of them." When Dean asks her how she even knows there is a God, she tells him, "We have to take it on faith."

That planted an idea in my head—what if there was no God? What if the angels were just as much in the dark as the rest of us? And what if Lucifer didn't rebel out of jealousy, but because he had learned the best-kept secret in all of Heaven?

I decided to run with it. When I started writing the *Luther Cross* series, I always knew that at some point, I would introduce Lucifer and this idea that God does not exist but the Divine Choir uses the myth of God to keep the angels in line. As I wrote those books, I seeded the potential for characters who could have their own spin-offs. Because in the world of indie publishing, series are important. But there comes a point when every series experiences a drop-off and it then becomes a case of diminishing returns. So having potential spin-offs is good to bring in new readers, keep existing readers engaged, and also to freshen things up for me as an author.

Lucifer wasn't initially a character I planned to do a spin-off of. But when I first introduced him in *Devil's Shadow*, I knew there was something about him that I would like to explore.

These books aren't the story of a man and his problematic relationship with his estranged father. There's already a fair bit of stories about the Devil that take that approach, and they're very good. Instead, I wanted to explore something different.

This is the story of a man trying to find his identity and his independence. It's about that pull between freedom and responsibility. And this is just the start.

Thank you again for taking a chance on this book. I hope you enjoyed it and that you'll be back for the next adventure.

Percival Constantine
December 2019
Kagoshima, Japan

ABOUT THE AUTHOR

Born and raised in the Chicagoland area, Percival Constantine grew up on a fairly consistent diet of superhero comics, action movies, video games, and TV shows. At the age of ten, he first began writing and has never really stopped.

Percival has been working in publishing since 2005 in various capacities—author, editor, formatter, letterer—and has written books, short stories, comics, and more. He has a Bachelor of Arts in English and Mass Media from Northeastern Illinois University and a Master of Arts in English and Screenwriting from Southern New Hampshire University. He currently resides in southern Japan, where he teaches literature and film while continuing to write.

MORNINGSTAR
BOOK 0
LUCIFER
FALLEN
PERCIVAL CONSTANTINE

VISIT PERCIVALCONSTANTINE.COM
FOR MORE THRILLING TALES!

Printed in Great Britain
by Amazon